BARBARA CARTLAND

Just Fate

Mandarin

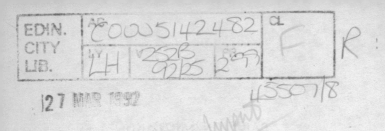

A Mandarin Paperback

JUST FATE

First published in Great Britain 1992
by Mandarin Paperbacks
Michelin House, 81 Fulham Road, London SW3 6RB

Mandarin is an imprint of the Octopus Publishing Group,
a division of Reed International Books Limited

A CIP catalogue record for this title
is available from the British Library
ISBN 0 7493 0800 1

Typeset by Falcon Typographic Art Ltd,
Edinburgh & London
Printed and bound in Great Britain
by Cox & Wyman Ltd, Reading, Berks

AUTHOR'S NOTE

Irish horses first became fashionable when Elisabeth Empress of Austria hunted in Ireland in 1880.

She was thrilled with the high-rising, high-jumping country and the horses which rivalled her own Hungarian Stud.

In 1907 an Irish horse named *Orby* won the English Derby, the Irish Derby and the Baldoyle Derby.

He was half-brother to *Rhodora* who, in 1908 won the One-Thousand Guineas Race.

Later, the Queen Mother's beautiful horse *Double Star* – starting in 1956 – ran fifty races in eight years, winning seventeen of them.

Double Star was a great favourite with the public. He was a very kind and placid horse and loved Lingfield where he was unbeatable, but disliked Cheltenham.

A good Trainer learns what type of track, ground, time of year and Jockey an outstanding horse prefers.

The Irish, whether they be man, woman or horse, are always sensitive, emotional and perceptive in their likes and dislikes.

CHAPTER ONE

Philomena walked back through the garden.

She was thinking how attractive it was and that it was a pity they could not afford more gardeners.

Since her father's death she and her mother had had to economise in a great number of ways.

Perhaps the one she minded most was that they now employed fewer gardeners and grooms in the stable.

Nevertheless the overgrown lawns, the yew-hedges that wanted clipping and the flower-beds which needed weeding were still lovely.

The flowers were a blaze of colour.

Philomena thought there was nothing lovelier than the time when the Spring flowers overlapped with the first roses of Summer.

It was her mother who had always paid most attention to the garden.

Her father, who had died last year, had been completely absorbed in his study of Greece.

Philomena sometimes thought he should be living there rather than in England.

However, if there was one thing her father was really proud of, it was his house and his name.

The Mansfordes were one of the oldest families in Great Britain.

The house, which had always been their family home, had been built in the reign of Queen Elizabeth.

Looking at it now ahead of her, Philomena thought nothing could be more beautiful.

The red bricks over the centuries had turned to a soft pink.

The strangely-shaped high chimneys were silhouetted against the blue sky, and the sun shone on the diamond-shaped panes of the casements.

She too loved her home.

Yet she thought with a little sigh that it was a difficult house to run without a large number of servants.

Since her father's death she had been in charge of everything.

Her mother, sweet, beautiful and very gentle, was quite incapable of organising anything.

That included her own life which had always been managed for her by her husband.

Being a masterful and in a way dominating man, that was what had attracted him to his wife in the first place.

Because they were the counterpart of each other they had been idyllically happy.

The only sorrow in Lionel Mansforde's life had been that he had had no son.

He had however been delighted with his two daughters and had chosen Greek names for them.

Their first daughter had been named Lais and their second Philomena.

It was inevitable, since she was small, fair and at the same time exquisitely lovely, that she should be called 'Mena'.

As her father had told her so often, 'Philomena' in Greek meant 'I am loved'.

"And that, my darling," he said firmly, "is what you will always be."

At the same time Mena knew that she had been in fact a disappointment to him.

There were four years between her and her sister.

Her mother had thought despairingly that she would have no more children after Lais was born.

Then when Elizabeth Mansforde learnt that she was once again pregnant, she had prayed fervently that it would be a son.

Instead Philomena had arrived.

However because she was so exquisite her father had almost forgotten his disappointment that she was not a boy.

"You are like a goddess from Olympus, my darling," he had said to her once.

"Perhaps that is what I am," Mena replied laughingly, "and I have come to you now simply because I fit so well into your research into the Glory that was Greece."

When there was any money to spare Lionel Mansforde spent it on pieces of Greek statuary and Greek vases.

Besides of course books of research or poetry written by those who had been privileged to visit the country.

He himself had been there once as a young man.

He had never forgotten how thrilled he had been by everything he had seen.

But it was about the Mansforde family and the house that he talked to his two daughters.

He described the deeds of heroism wrought by many whose name he bore.

The part they had played at the battles of Agincourt and of Worcester.

He spoke of the distinguished Mansforde who had become one of Marlborough's Generals.

"It is sad for Papa that he has not a son to be a Hero like the one he was telling us about this morning," Mena said.

"I know, darling," her mother replied in her soft voice, "and that is why you must try to make up for what he had missed by giving him as much love and attention as possible."

Mena had known exactly what her mother meant, but Lais had said:

"I think Papa should be grateful to have us. After all, we are both very pretty!"

She had just become conscious of her beauty because the choir-boys stared at her in Church.

And when she came into a room, her father and mother's friends would break off their conversation to stare at her with undisguised admiration.

It was, Mena thought sadly, Lais's beauty that had taken her away and made her forget all about them.

Mena was very happy and loved being with her mother.

Yet she sometimes thought it would be fun to have somebody of her own age to laugh with and enjoy a joke.

Her mother did not find jokes very funny.

In fact since her husband's death she had become listless and not particularly interested in anything.

Mena thought despairingly that it was difficult to think of anything she could do to make her mother happier.

"She depended so much on Papa," she told herself,

"and misses not only his love and attention, but also having a man about the house and knowing she must make herself look lovely for him."

At forty-two Elizabeth Mansforde was still a very beautiful woman.

She had been breath-takingly lovely when her husband had married her when she was the same age as Mena was now.

Wherever they went people flattered her and congratulated him.

She had blossomed under their appreciation like a rose coming into bloom.

'That is exactly what Mama is like,' Mina thought as she walked towards the house, 'a flower.'

But it was a flower that was fading simply because Elizabeth Mansforde felt that nobody was interested in her.

'Now that we are out of mourning,' Mena thought 'Perhaps we should give some parties.'

She tried to think who in the neighbourhood they could ask.

There were a great number of married couples.

Yet she could not think of a single man who could balance her mother at luncheons or dinners.

There were just a few young men of her own age.

However as they had been in deep mourning for a year there was always the chance that new people had come into the neighbourhood without her being aware of it.

'I must do something about Mama!' she thought firmly as she walked into the house.

She walked across the hall, from which rose a fine oak staircase with exquisitely carved newels.

She went into the Sitting-Room.

This was one of the loveliest rooms in the house.

It had a low ceiling, two large bow windows and a very fine marble mantelpiece which had been added later to the original fireplace.

Mrs. Mansforde was sitting in the window on a sofa.

It had been drawn forward so that the sun shining through the diamond-paned windows turned her hair to shining gold.

It was the same colour as her daughter's, and so was the pink and white translucence of her skin.

Mena's eyes were a deeper blue than her mother's, which now always looked sad and despondent.

She looked up as her daughter approached her.

"Have you enjoyed your walk, Mena?" she enquired.

"I went into the fields and back through the woods,' Mena replied, "and look, Mama, I have brought you some wild orchids. I knew you would be pleased because they are so lovely."

Mrs Mansforde took them from her.

"They are very pretty," she agreed. "We used to grow orchids in the greenhouse when we had enough gardeners to take care of them."

"Yes, I know, Mama, and I remember how lovely you looked when once you wore them in your hair for a dinner-party."

Unexpectedly her mother laughed.

"I remember that party," she said. "The other ladies present wearing their tiaras were furious because the gentlemen were all paying me compliments and ignoring their diamonds."

"You came to say good-night to me," Mena recalled, "and I thought you looked like a Fairy Princess."

"And that was how I felt because your father was with me," Mrs. Mansforde answered.

14

Now the sadness was back in her eyes.

Mena picked up the wild orchids and added them to one of the vases filled with flowers on a side-table.

"I was thinking, Mama," she said, "that now we are out of mourning we must give some parties."

"Parties?" Mrs. Mansforde asked. "Why should we do that?"

"Because it would be pleasant to see our neighbours again," Mena replied. "I was thinking of all those people like Sir Rupert and Lady Hall who used to come here quite often when Papa was alive."

Her mother did not say anything and Mena went on:

"Then there is Colonel and Mrs. Strangeways who I am sure would like to see you again."

"But how can we give a party if your father is not here to play host?" her mother asked. "You know it would not be the same without him at the head of the table being so witty and amusing."

There were tears in her voice and Mena said hastily:

"I thought too, Mama, that we might have new gowns. The fashion has of course changed a little during this last year when we have been wearing black."

There was a pause before Mrs. Mansforde said in a helpless tone:

"If you want to have a party, dearest, then you must arrange it. You know your father always organised everything like that and I would not know where to begin."

"I will arrange it, Mama," Mena said, "and I am sure it will cheer you up. I know Mrs. Johnson is longing to have somebody admire her cooking."

Mrs. Johnson had been in the house ever since Mena could remember.

She was a very good cook.

She had been driven to despair when nothing she sent to the table could tempt her mistress into eating more than two or three mouthfuls.

"I am not really hungry, darling," she would say to Mena when she remonstrated with her. "I remember how particular your father was about having interesting dishes, but I only pretended to enjoy them in order to please him."

'I must think of a way to make Mama more interested in life,' Mina thought.

She had already tried to interest her mother in books that she had sent down from London to add to the Library.

It was already a very large one.

But Elizabeth Mansforde had never been a great reader.

When her husband had read aloud to her what he had written about Greece she had always seemed very attentive.

But Mena has thought secretly that she was listening to his voice rather than to what he said.

Now she was determined to do something to rouse her mother from her apathy.

She went to the Queen Anne *secretaire* which stood in the corner of the Drawing-Room and started to write down a list of their neighbours.

It was rather depressing to think how old they all were.

She had always thought of her mother as being a young woman.

Her father, who had been only a few years older, had often said:

"The trouble with this County is that the young go to London and leave all the 'Old Fogies' behind!"

Even so, when he was alive there had always seemed to be people coming and going in the house.

Many of them, Mena knew, came to ask his advice about horses.

Her father had been an outstanding rider. He had also known a great deal about horseflesh.

Anyone in the neighbourhood when buying horses invariably consulted him before they completed a deal.

Mena had been only seventeen and still busy having an extensive education when her father had died.

She was aware that because he had no son he was determined that she should be unusually well-educated for a girl.

It was due perhaps to a selfish desire to have somebody with whom he could discuss his academic interests.

It was something he could not do with his wife.

As Mena knew, her mother listened attentively and praised everything he said.

At the same time he must have been aware that she had no critical faculty.

She was in fact not interested in the subject he was discussing, but only in him.

He adored her.

Nevertheless he longed for someone with whom he could have a debate.

Someone who had the intelligence to hold and voice a different opinion from his own.

He found this in his daughter Mena.

He had therefore insisted that she should be educated as if she was a boy.

She had Tutors and Governesses not only in the usual subjects but also in stranger ones like Oriental Languages and Eastern Religions.

17

Of course she had a special Tutor to teach her the History of Ancient Greece.

To Mena it was entrancing.

Not only because she was genuinely interested in what she learnt, but also because it so delighted her father.

She often thought that if her mother's life had collapsed at his death, so had hers.

It was agony to go into his Study knowing he would not be there.

How often she had run to him excitedly to tell him of something she had read in a book, or a newspaper.

"Look, Papa, what I have just read! A Temple has been discovered dedicated to Apollo on one of the Greek islands!"

Her father's eyes would light up.

"Where have they found that?" he would ask. "I cannot remember hearing that before!"

He would then be as excited as if Mena had found a valuable jewel.

If her mother missed the love which her husband had given her, Mena missed the stimulus to her mind and her imagination.

She often felt as if her father's death had drawn a dark curtain down in front of her.

She still had no idea how to penetrate it.

She had written down half-a-dozen names when, to her surprise, she heard voices in the hall.

For a moment she thought she must be imagining things.

No one had called on them for so long with the exception of the Vicar, who was an old man.

There had also been Mena's Tutors, although she

18

had dismissed them a month ago when she became eighteen.

She had wanted to continue her studies simply because her lessons filled the long days.

But she had realised it was an unnecessary extravagance.

They could not afford it, and anyway she had reached the point where there was really no more her Tutors could teach her.

"I must teach myself now," she said sternly.

She knew that was not the same as having somebody with whom to discuss the subject.

Or when her father had been alive, to argue about it.

Now she could hear the sound of Johnson's – the Butler's – voice and another voice which for the moment she could not distinguish.

Then the Drawing-Room door opened and Johnson announced:

"Lady Barnham, M'am!"

Mrs. Mansforde looked up in astonishment and Mena gave a cry.

"Lais – is it really you?"

A vision of elegance came into the room.

Lais had always been lovely, Mena thought.

But in a fashionable gown with its skirt drawn to the back in a bustle and a hat trimmed with green feathers she was breath-taking.

She walked across the room towards her mother.

Mrs. Mansforde held out both her hands to her.

"Lais, my dearest! What a surprise! I thought you had forgotten all about us!"

"It is lovely to see you, Mama," Lais said.

She bent and gave her mother a light kiss on the cheek.

Then she turned towards Mena who had run across the room to her side.

"Good Heavens, Mena!" she exclaimed. "You have grown up! I was still thinking of you as a little girl."

It seemed extraordinary, Mena thought, that Lais had not been home for four years.

Yet she still had that sharp note in her voice there had been before she left.

When Lais was eighteen her Godmother, who was both rich and distinguished, had offered to present her at Court.

"*I will give Lais a Season in London*," she wrote.

Lais had been wildly excited at the prospect.

Her father and mother had been extremely grateful to the Countess of Winterton for being so generous and so thoughtful.

Mr. Mansforde had no wish to go to London even for a few months.

But he knew that his beautiful daughter should have her chance to appear in the Social World, which she would undoubtedly 'take by storm'.

He had known that to leave home would disrupt the happiness he and his wife found together in the quietness of the country.

It was therefore with a sigh of relief he learned Lais could make her début with her Godmother.

By the end of the season Lais had outshone every other débutante.

It was then she announced that she was going to marry Lord Barnham.

Mena had thought it very exciting until she met the prospective Bridegroom.

To her Lord Barnham seemed old and very pompous.

Somewhat tentatively she had asked her sister:

20

"Are you really in love with him, Lais?"

Lais, who had been regarding her reflection in the mirror, replied:

"He is very rich, has a very important position at Court, and the tiara I shall wear amongst the Peeresses at the Opening of Parliament is absolutely dazzling!"

It was not an answer to the question Mena had put to her.

Yet she had known that no matter what the family might say Lais intended to marry Lord Barnham.

Lais had said before she left home that she thought they lived in 'the back of beyond'.

She had been determined to marry somebody important.

Mena's head on the contrary had been filled with romantic stories of love which she associated with a 'Knight in Shining Armour' who slew a dragon to save a lovely Princess.

There were also gallants who climbed up the side of a house to reach the balcony on which they could steal a kiss from a beautiful damsel.

She could not imagine Lord Barnham performing either of those exploits.

But if he was what Lais wanted, that was what she would have.

Lais's wedding, which was spectacular, had taken place in London.

"I should have thought that Lais might have married from here," Mena had said to her father. "The garden is so lovely in the Summer and Mrs. Johnson is so disappointed that she will not be baking the wedding-cake."

Instead they had travelled to London to stay with Lady Winterton.

She had already booked St. George's Church in

21

Hanover Square for the ceremony and arranged for the reception to take place in her house.

It had been one of the most important weddings of the year.

Every pew was packed with smart and distinguished people.

Lais had moved up the aisle on her father's arm wearing a gown which Mena thought must have cost a 'King's Ransom'.

She had thought that every woman in the congregation was looking at her sister either critically or with envy.

When they had returned to the country her father had said:

"Now we can get back to doing something really interesting. I have never listened to so much inane conversation and boring platitudes as I have these last few days!"

Mena laughed.

"You are being very censorious, Papa!"

"And with reason," her father replied. "I find it extraordinary that any daughter of mine should tolerate anything so tedious!"

Mena did not answer.

She was thinking that her sister would not find it tedious, in fact very much the opposite.

The night before the wedding, when she had gone to Lais's bed-room to say good-night, her sister had said:

"Think how important I am going to be, Mena, and think how rich George is. I can have the smartest gowns in the whole of London, and when we do have to go to the country, I will fill the house with George's friends who are all as distinguished as he is!"

"Will you not . . find them a little . . old?" Mena had asked hesitatingly.

"I find them socially important – and that is all that matters!" Lais replied.

Mena had watched her sister drive away on her honeymoon with Lord Barnham.

She found as she looked at him that he made her shiver.

How could Lais, who was so lovely, possibly be in love with a man who looked old enough to be her father?

He was already beginning to go bald.

Mena could not help wondering if Lais would feel differently about him when she came back from her honeymoon.

But she never got the chance to ask her.

The extraordinary fact was that from the moment she married Lais, to all intents and purposes, disappeared.

She sent her father and mother presents at Christmas.

There was also something small and rather trivial for Mena.

She wrote letters to them very occasionally and answered one out of a dozen they wrote to her.

Then Lord Mansforde died unexpectedly during a very cold Winter in which he had developed pneumonia.

Mena had thought that Lais would at least come to the Funeral.

Instead she sent a very large and expensive wreath.

With it was a letter explaining that Lord Barnham and she had been invited to Sandringham for a shoot.

She was sure her mother would understand that she could not refuse to be a guest of the Prince of Wales.

It was quite an affectionate letter.

At the same time, Mena could not help thinking that Lais was relieved to have a good excuse for not coming home.

23

And yet incredibly, now, when she least expected it, Lais had appeared.

Looking, Mena thought, lovelier than she had ever seen her.

There was very little resemblance between the sisters.

Lais had taken after her father's side of the family.

Her hair was dark, while her eyes were astonishingly blue, like her mother's.

The contrast startled everyone who saw her and any man who looked at her always looked again.

She was very elegant, taller than Mena, and she had a grace which might have been Greek.

Moreover, as if in sympathy with her father's obsession, she had perfect classical features.

Dressed in the very latest fashion with jewels sparkling in her ears and at her throat Mena could only stare at her.

She found it hard to believe she was real.

"If I have grown older, Lais," she said, "you have grown even more beautiful than you were before."

Lais smiled.

"That is what everybody says," she replied, "and now, like you, I am out of mourning, and I intend to enjoy myself."

"Out of mourning?" Mrs. Mansforde repeated. "What are you saying?"

"Really, mother, do you never read the newspapers?" Lais asked. "Surely you are aware that George died just a month after Papa?"

"I had no idea of it!" her mother answered. "Oh, my dear, I am so sorry."

"Why did you not write and tell us?" Mena asked.

"There was no need for you to make a fuss about it," Lais said sharply. "George was buried in Yorkshire where his family house is situated, and it would have been quite unnecessary for Mama to travel all that way for the Funeral!"

"I am sorry, so very sorry," Mrs. Mansforde said gently. "You must have been very unhappy."

"Yes – of course," Lais said quickly. "But there is no sense in drooling over the past, and one has to look forward to the future."

"I feel there is no – future for me," her mother said with a little sob.

"I can understand that," Lais said, "but as far as I am concerned, my future is very important, and that is why I am here."

She sat down in an arm-chair as she spoke.

Mena sat on the end of the sofa on which her mother was lying.

"You will realise, I am sure, Mama," Lais went on, "that now I am no longer in mourning I have to think about myself very seriously."

Mrs. Mansforde looked surprised, but Mena asked:

"Where have you been since your husband died? If you could not entertain or go to parties, why did you not come home?"

"Come back here?" Lais asked in surprise. "Why should I do that?"

"I just thought," Mena said a little abashed, "that you might have wanted to see us."

"I had a better idea than that," Lais replied. "I have some friends who live in France, so I went first to their Château in the country, then to Paris."

Mena gave a little gasp.

It was something she had never thought of anyone doing when they were bereaved.

She realised from the way her sister spoke that there

was no need for restrictions or for people to be surprised if she enjoyed herself.

"Now that I am back," Lais was saying, "I have come to tell you that I intend to marry the Duke of Kernthorpe."

Mena drew in her breath and her mother said:

"I am so glad, my dearest, that you have found somebody who will make you happy."

"Very happy," Lais agreed.

"And you are going to marry him at once?" Mena asked.

She wondered as she spoke if it was not really too soon after the death of Lord Barnham.

There was a pause before Lais said:

"Nothing is arranged yet. In fact, to be honest, the Duke has not yet asked me to be his wife."

Mrs. Mansforde looked at her daughter.

"But – you said . ."

"What I said, Mama," Lais interrupted, "is that I *intend* to marry him, and it is only a question of time before he proposes."

There was silence before Lais went on:

"We have seen quite a lot of each other, and where do you think I am staying at the moment?"

Mena thought quickly, then exclaimed:

"Kerne Castle!"

"Of course! And that is why I was able to drive here to see you."

When making out her list of neighbours Mena had not thought of Kerne Castle or the Duke of Kernthorpe.

He had never been a friend of her father's, in fact she could not remember ever having met him.

Of course she was aware that Kerne Castle was only seven miles away.

26

Most people in the county spoke of the Duke with bated breath.

He was obviously very important, but he also, as people said 'kept himself to himself'.

He played little part in County affairs.

He was more concerned with his position in London and with his race-horses at Newmarket.

He also, she knew, had a hunting-lodge in Leicestershire.

"It used to be different in the old days!" Mena had heard people complain. "T'Old Duke were a very congenial man, an' the Duchess always opened the Flower Show and gave a Garden Party in the summer."

The present Duke was a stranger to them and Mena wondered if, like Lais, he found this part of the country dull.

Almost as if she had asked the question her sister answered it.

"The Duke has not spent much time at Kerne Castle," she said, "and now that I have seen it, I do not blame him for preferring London and his other houses."

"It would be delightful to have you living so near us, dearest," Mrs. Mansforde said gently.

"Well, I am here now," Lais went on, as if what her mother had said was immaterial, "to ask you, Mama, to come and stay at Kerne Castle and meet the Duke."

Her mother stared at her in astonishment.

"But surely," she said after a moment, "he can come here?"

"Do not be stupid, Mama!" Lais exclaimed. "He has a large house-party and I can hardly drag him away just to meet you! When I told him how old our house was and to what a distinguished family I belong, he said unexpectedly that he would like to meet my mother."

"That is very kind of him," Mrs. Mansforde said.

"Kind?" Lais questioned, "it is not a question of kindness, Mama. You have to understand that the Duke is making sure that his next wife is the right person for the great position he can offer her."

"His *next* wife?" Mena exclaimed.

"Of course he has been married before!" Lais said sharply as if her sister was being very stupid. "He was married when he was quite young to a woman chosen for him by his parents because they considered her eminently suitable for their son. I gather, although he rarely speaks of it, that the marriage was not happy and his wife died having a miscarriage."

Mrs. Mansforde made an expression of sympathy and Lais went on:

"Of course, I can give him an heir, which is what he needs, and I am quite certain, having looked at the portraits, that I will be the most beautiful of all the Duchesses who have preceded me."

"Of course you will!" Mena said. "At the same time, it seems strange that Papa never knew the Duke. How old is he?"

There was a little pause before Lais replied:

"I suppose anyone can look it up in the Peerage, but I think he is about forty-five."

Mena stared at her sister in astonishment before she said:

"But surely, dearest, that is rather old for you?"

"Really, Mena, do not be so foolish!" Lais said. "What has age to do with it? And William is still a very attractive man."

She glanced at the clock over the mantelpiece and said:

"I must be getting back. The Duke has gone riding

28

with some of the other members of the party, and I must be there when they return."

She rose to her feet and continued:

"I will send a carriage for you, Mama, at about two o'clock to-morrow afternoon so that you will arrive at the Castle in time for tea. Wear your prettiest gown and bring every jewel you possess."

Mrs. Mansforde looked a little bewildered. Then she asked:

"What about Mena?"

"Oh – Mena!" Lais exclaimed. "Surely, she can stay here?"

"Of course she cannot!" her mother answered. "She would be alone, and I am sure you want her to come with me."

The silence was so obvious that Mena said:

"I shall be . . quite all right . . here. How long is Mama going to . . stay at the Castle?"

"I thought until Monday," Lais replied. "That is when most of the guests will be going back to London."

"I cannot come without Mena, dearest!" Mrs. Mansforde said.

She spoke in a firmer voice than she usually used and Mena looked at her in surprise.

"I will be all right, Mama," Mena said again.

Mrs. Mansforde shook her head.

"Your father would not have allowed that, and there is no time to find anyone else to stay here with you."

"You are making it very difficult for me," Lais said. "I have not told the Duke that I have a sister, although I have often said how lonely I feel now that Papa is dead."

There was silence.

Then because Mena felt it was embarrassing she said:

29

"Perhaps I could . . come with Mama and . . look after her . . and no one . . need know that I am . . your sister."

She thought there was a sudden light in Lais's eyes as she went on:

"I could be her . . Companion . . then there would be no need for me to eat in the Dining-Room . . but I could be with Mama when you did not . . want her."

"That is a splendid idea!" Lais said after a moment's silence.

"I want Mena with me," Mrs. Mansforde said, "and I cannot understand why you have not told the Duke that you have a sister!"

"It would take too long to explain that to you, and now I have to go," Lais replied. "If Mena will act as your Companion, then there will be no difficulties about her staying in the castle."

She walked towards the door and Mena followed her.

As they went into the hall Lais said in a low voice:

"Mama does not understand, but I am playing my cards very carefully. I want to marry the Duke – I am determined to marry him. So please, Mena, help me, and do not make it any more difficult for me than it is at the moment."

Mena's heart melted.

"Of course I will help you, Lais. I want you to be happy. And, as you have already said, you will be the most beautiful Duchess there has ever been!"

Lais smiled at her.

"Thank you, Mena," she said. "I have a lot of clothes I can give you which I wore before I went into mourning. I might have thought of it before, but there was such a commotion, with George dying when

30

he did and the family being unpleasant because he left me all his money."

"So you are rich! Oh, dearest, how wonderful!" Mena exclaimed.

"It was only when I was shopping in Paris that I realised that because Papa was dead you might be hard up."

"Things have been a little difficult," Mena admitted, "but we managed."

"I will give you some money if you keep the Duke from knowing you are my sister just while Mama is at the Castle. And I promise as soon as I get back to London I will send you the clothes."

"Thank you, Lais," Mena said. "That is very kind of you."

Lais put her hand on her sister's shoulder then as an after-thought kissed her cheek.

"You do understand," she said, "that I have to marry the Duke. But I assure you there is a great deal of competition."

"You will win, of course you will win!" Mena said, "and I will be very, very careful that no one guesses that I am your sister. After all, we are not a bit alike!"

"That is exactly what I was thinking," Lais agreed.

She walked towards the door.

Old Johnson was outside talking to the coachman.

Mena noticed that the four horses which drew the carriage in which Lais had arrived were perfectly matched and superbly bred.

She wanted to go out and pat them and talk to the coachman.

She thought however that might be a mistake in case when he returned to the Castle he mentioned her to the other servants.

As Lais went down the steps and was assisted into the carriage by a footman, she moved back into the hall.

She knew that she would not be noticed.

She thought perhaps Lais would wave to her as the horses moved off.

But her sister merely leaned back against the cushioned seat and Mena watched the carriage out of sight.

Then she ran back into the Drawing-Room.

Her mother was still reclining on the sofa where she had left her.

"You are going to Kerne Castle, Mama!" she said. "Is that not exciting!"

"I was just thinking," Mrs. Mansforde replied, "how different I would feel if your father were with me. Oh, Mena I do miss him terribly!"

CHAPTER TWO

"You cannot go to the Castle dressed all in black, Mama!" Mena declared.

"What does it matter?" her mother asked. "I am only going to please Lais."

"Lais will be annoyed if you do not look lovely," Mena said sternly.

She searched for the clothes her mother had worn before her husband's death.

They had been tidily packed away.

When she found them, she knew they were exactly what her mother should wear while she was at the Castle.

Her father, being proud of his wife, had always been particular that she should look beautiful.

He insisted that every gown she wore was not only becoming but also made of good material.

Her afternoon and evening gowns were consequently just as fresh and attractive as they had been when they were new.

Despite her mother's protests, Mena had insisted on her trying on a number of garments she had forgotten she had.

When the carriage arrived, Mrs. Mansforde was looking

ravishing in a gown she had bought for an important occasion.

It was for a County meeting at which her husband had specially wanted to show her off.

When Mena had re-trimmed her hat she thought Lais could not be anything but proud of her mother.

"It is ridiculous your coming with me as my Companion instead of as my daughter," Mrs. Mansforde kept saying.

"Do not worry about it, Mama," Mena pleaded. "All I want is to see the Castle and, if possible, the Duke's horses. And you know how disagreeable Lais will be if she does not get her own way."

Mrs. Mansforde sighed.

"I am sure that is true, but when a woman is as beautiful as Lais, it is impossible for her not to think she is a Queen in her own right."

Mena laughed.

"That is exactly what Lais is, so let her marry her King, even if he is only a Duke. Then we need not worry about her any more."

She thought as she spoke that they had had little chance of worrying about Lais in the last four years.

She knew the way Lais had cut herself off from her family had distressed both her father and her mother.

Mena was impressed by the carriage when it arrived.

It was similar to the one in which Lais had come the day before, but had a team of almost white horses.

"I feel like *Cinderella* going to the Ball," she told her mother. "All I need is a Fairy Godmother to wave her magic wand over me!"

Mrs. Mansforde looked at her critically as if for the first time.

"You look very lovely . . my dearest," she said, "but do you not think your hat is too plain?"

"You have forgotten, Mama," Mena said, "I am your Companion. That is why I took off the flowers because I thought they were too frivolous."

Mrs. Mansforde looked upset and Mena said quickly:

"Now do not worry about me, Mama. Just make yourself charming to the Duke, and when we come home on Monday we can laugh about everything that has happened."

There was silence for a few minutes.

Then she said:

"You must not forget, Mama, to refer to me, if it is necessary, as 'Miss Johnson'."

"'Miss Johnson'?" her mother exclaimed in astonishment. "Why should I do that?"

Slowly and laboriously Mena explained that if anyone asked who she was she could not have the same name as her mother.

It took her a little time to make her mother understand how important it was that no one should notice her.

Then finally Mrs. Mansforde said:

"But, Johnson – why Johnson?"

Mena laughed.

"It was the first name I could think of that sounded dull and prosaic, and I thought that, if the servants talked about Mr. Johnson, people might assume I was a relation of his."

Her mother gave a cry of protest.

"Of course they must not think that! Oh, dearest, why do we have to carry out this ridiculous charade of Lais's? It is wrong – quite wrong – and I am sure your father would be most displeased."

35

Mena knew that was true.

Her father had been very proud of his name and his antecedents. He would not think it at all amusing that his younger daughter was using the name of his man-servant.

Because she thought it had upset her mother she said:

"If it makes you feel happier, Mama, I will change it. What name do you suggest?"

There was silence until her mother said:

"Why not Ford? We will easily remember it because it is part of our name, and it will not seem quite so wrong as using the name of one of our servants."

Mena though it was very clever of her mother to think of it.

She therefore said:

"Of course, Mama, I will call myself 'Miss Ford'. But you may be sure that the Duke's guests will not even know that I exist."

"It is wrong – I know it is wrong!" Mrs. Mansforde persisted.

Because she did not want her mother to be upset Mena talked to her of other things as they drove on towards the Castle.

She herself was very excited at the idea of seeing it for the first time.

At breakfast her mother had said:

"I remember now going with your father to the Castle soon after we were married."

"Oh, Mama, you did not say so to Lais!" Mena exclaimed.

"It was a long time ago," Mrs. Mansforde went on. "Your father had been asked to dinner to meet the

36

Ambassador of Greece because the old Duke knew he was interested in that country."

"I am sure Papa was thrilled," Mena remarked. "Tell me – what was the Castle like?"

"I am afraid I can hardly remember it, but I recall driving there with your father and the lovely things he said to me when we were going home."

There was a note in her voice that Mena always dreaded.

It meant that looking back into the past would inevitably bring on tears.

"When we get to the Castle," she said quickly, "you must try to find out why the Duke comes there so seldom, and why he apparently has no interest in the affairs of the County. To me it seems rather strange."

"I know your father would think it most neglectful," her mother replied. "He always said that 'Absentee Landlords' were a great mistake, and no one could expect workmen to do their best if their employers were not there to criticise or give praise when it is due."

Mena smiled.

"That sounds just like Papa, and it is what he did himself."

"He would be very upset if he saw the garden now," Mrs. Mansforde said sadly. "I do wish we could afford another gardener."

"So do I," Mena agreed. "But you know, Mama, it would be impossible to keep the horses too, and I could not bear to have nothing to ride, and you would miss being able to go out in the carriage."

Mrs. Mansforde sighed, but she did not go on arguing.

As Mena thought, she accepted things as they were

because she felt too limp to suggest ways of improving them.

Finally the horses turned in through two huge ornamental iron gates tipped with gold.

They then moved down a drive bordered by ancient oak trees.

Mena craned her neck to have her first glimpse of the Castle.

When she saw it she realised it was even more magnificent than she had anticipated.

With its huge tower on which was flying the Duke's standard it was exactly how she thought a Castle should look.

The horses drew up with a flourish at the bottom of a flight of stone steps which led up to an impressive front door.

As they came to a standstill footmen ran down a red carpet before they opened the carriage-door.

Mrs. Mansforde stepped out.

Mena, carrying her mother's jewel-case, walked behind her.

At the top of the steps a Butler bowed.

"Good-afternoon, M'am," he said. "I hope you had a pleasant journey?"

"Very pleasant, thank you," Mrs. Mansforde answered.

"Her Ladyship's waiting for you, M'am in the Drawing-Room, and the Housekeeper will look after your Companion, if she will kindly go to the top of the stairs."

Her mother gave Mena what she thought was almost a despairing look.

With an obvious effort she followed the Butler while Mena obediently went up the staircase.

The Housekeeper in rustling black silk with the

silver chatelaine at her waist greeted her pleasantly.

"I hope you're not too tired after your journey," she said. "I always find travelling any distance gives me a headache."

"I enjoyed it," Mena replied, "and the horses managed the distance surprisingly quickly!"

"They go too quick for my liking!" the Housekeeper remarked. "It's all too easy to have an accident in those narrow lanes."

She showed Mena into what she saw was a very pleasant room.

It was naturally not one which would have been offered to any of the Duke's personal guests.

"I think you'll be comfortable here," the House-keeper said, "and I'll show you where your Lady is sleeping."

They walked for some distance to where an impos-ing and beautiful room had been allotted to Mrs. Mansforde.

Mena found it had a Sitting-Room opening out of it.

"Lady Barnham suggested you'd like to have your meals in here," the Housekeeper said.

"I hope it is not too inconvenient," Mena said apologetically.

"It'll be quite easy to arrange," the Housekeeper replied, "though, as it happens, His Grace's guests don't often bring their Companions with them."

Mena felt she ought to apologise for her mother doing anything so unusual, but the Housekeeper went on:

"Lady's-maids are of course to be expected, but I understand Mrs. Mansforde's isn't well at the moment."

Mena felt relieved and at the same time amused.

She knew at once that this was Lais's invention since her mother might not seem so important if she did not have a Lady's-maid.

"I can look after Mrs. Mansforde," she said.

"There's no need for you to do that," the House-keeper replied. "I've already arranged for one of the Senior Housemaids who I'm sure will give every satisfaction to wait on her."

"That is very kind of you," Mena said.

She looked into her mother's Sitting-Room which she could see was lavishly furnished.

There was a glass-fronted cabinet containing a number of books.

They would be a delight, Mena thought, while she was staying at the Castle.

She was also anxious to see the Castle itself and its contents as well as the grounds.

The quick glimpse she had through the windows had already told her that the gardens were beautifully kept.

She knew her mother would be thrilled by them.

The luggage was being brought up by footmen.

She therefore went back to her own room to find that she too had been allotted a housemaid to do her unpacking.

'Everything is certainly very comfortable,' she thought.

She hoped her mother would enjoy it all.

Mena had looked after her at home, and the Johnsons did their best in a house that was far too big for them.

She was sure her mother would enjoy a household where everything ran on well-oiled wheels.

There were well-trained servants to do everything that was required.

She had taken off her hat and the light jacket she

wore over her gown when a footman knocked on the door. He informed her that tea was waiting for her in her mother's Sitting-Room.

She thanked him and found when she reached it that a delicious tea had been brought up.

There were cakes that would have made Mrs. Johnson jealous.

She ate quite a lot of everything that had been provided.

She was standing looking out of the window when she heard her mother being shown into the bed-room next door.

She waited until she was alone, then went through the communicating door.

"Oh, there you are, Mena darling!" her mother exclaimed.

It was exactly what Mena had been afraid she would say when the Housekeeper was within hearing.

"Be careful, Mama!" she warned. "You must not forget that I am 'Miss Ford'."

"I had forgotten," her mother said. "Oh, dear, why can we not just be ourselves?"

"Tell me what is happening downstairs," Mena said.

"There are already quite a number of people here," Mrs Mansforde said, "and they all seem very pleasant. One of them – I did not catch his name – said he had known Papa."

"That was lovely for you!" Mena smiled.

She helped her mother off with her hat, then undid the gown she was wearing.

"I am going to rest before dinner," Mrs. Mansforde said.

"You have not yet told me what the Duke is like," Mena reminded her.

"He is out riding, so I have not met him. But Lais was very sweet and introduced me to all her friends who told me how much they admired her."

Mena helped her mother finish undressing and got her into bed.

"Now try to sleep, Mama," she said, "and I will wake you in plenty of time so that there will be no rush."

"Thank you, darling," Mrs. Mansforde murmured and shut her eyes.

Mena went into the Sitting-Room and stood for a long time at the window.

She wondered, if Lais became the Duchess, whether she would appreciate the beauty of the gardens, the woods that lay behind them, and of course the great Castle itself.

"I must see everything I can," she told herself.

She then thought that when everybody was at dinner there would be time for her to explore the gardens.

She wondered when she could expect her own dinner to be brought to her.

An hour later Mena woke her mother who had been sound asleep.

All she could think of was making her look as beautiful as she had been in the old days when she had gone out with her father.

She had chosen for the first night a gown she had last worn at the Hunt Ball. After it her father had declared she eclipsed every other woman present.

Fortunately her mother had forgotten this occasion on which he had been particularly proud of her.

She allowed Mena to dress her hair and choose what jewellery she should wear.

"I think it would be a mistake, Mama, to wear your tiara this evening," Mena said. "I have always understood that the first night when people have just arrived is not the smartest evening."

"Yes, of course, you are right about that, dearest," Mrs. Mansforde agreed. "And I would not wish to look over-dressed."

It was at that moment that Lais came into the room.

"Are you ready, Mama?" she asked. "I thought perhaps you would like me to go with you downstairs."

"Thank you, dearest," her mother said. "I have never gone down without your father before."

Lais was not listening, but looking round the room to make sure there was no maid there.

"Are you all right, Mena? They are looking after you?"

"Yes," Mena replied, "and I know I have you to thank for it."

"I made it quite clear that you would have your meals in Mama's *Boudoir*," Lais said.

Mrs. Mansforde looked horrified.

"Oh, but surely Mena can come down to dinner? I cannot bear to think of her sitting up here all by herself."

Lais frowned and Mena said quickly:

"Of course that would be impossible, Mama. It has all been arranged, and you know how uncomfortable I should feel with the guests looking down their noses at me because I am earning my living."

Mrs. Mansforde would have protested, but Lais said:

"Now, do not fuss, Mama. I have arranged that Mena will be very comfortable. All you have to remember is that she is your Companion."

She turned to Mena to ask:

"I suppose you have given yourself another name. I forgot about it yesterday when I came over to the house."

"I thought of it!" Mena replied, "and Mama wants to call me 'Miss Ford'."

"But, surely . . ?" Lais began.

"It will be easy for her to remember," Mena pointed out, "and if somebody thinks I am a poor relation – what does it matter?"

"I suppose not," Lais said reluctantly. "Anyway, if you keep out of sight, nobody is likely to ask who you are."

"No, of course not," Mena smiled.

Lais looked at her mother.

"I like that gown, Mama. You look very pretty in it!"

"That is what Mena said," her mother replied.

"I was just getting Mama's jewellery out," Mena said, "but I thought her tiara would be better left until to-morrow night."

"Good gracious, has she still got it?" Lais asked. "I thought it would have been sold by now."

Mena gave her a meaningful glance.

"Papa saved for a long time to buy that tiara for Mama," she said, "and it would break her heart to part with it."

Lais did not answer, she was looking in the jewel-case and, Mena thought, disparaging its contents.

"I thought I would put Mama's two little diamond stars in her hair," Mena suggested.

"Yes, do that," Lais agreed, "and she could wear her necklace, although it is not a very large one."

Mena remembered that as a child she had always thought it enormous, but knew it would be a mistake to say so.

44

Finally when she had finished and the jewel-box was half empty Mrs. Mansforde was ready to go down-stairs.

She looked very lovely and very ladylike beside Lais who was as colourful as a peacock.

Her gown was emerald green which accentuated the darkness of her hair and the whiteness of her skin.

She wore a necklace of emeralds and a bandeau on her forehead of emeralds and diamonds.

There were bracelets to match and ear-rings which glittered every time she moved.

She looked at herself in the mirror with satisfaction before she said:

"Come along, Mama! The Duke is longing to meet you and I think he is going to be impressed with both of us."

"I hope so, dearest," Mrs. Mansforde said. "I would not wish to let you down."

Lais did not speak.

Mena bent forward to kiss her mother on the cheek.

"You look very beautiful, Mama, and I know every-body downstairs will tell you so."

Mrs. Mansforde smiled at her.

"Good-night, my darling," she said, "do not wait up for me. The housemaid will help me undress."

"I will be awake, and I will help you," Mena prom-ised.

Lais was already outside in the corridor waiting impatiently.

As they walked down the corridor to the top of the Grand Staircase Mena slipped back into the bed-room.

It would be a mistake for any of the other guests to see her.

It was only a minute or so before two housemaids came into the room to tidy it.

"I am going next door," Mena told them. "Have you any idea what time I shall have my dinner?"

"I understands a footman's bringin' it up now," one of the maids replied. "It's sure to be late before they finishes in th' Dining-Room."

"That is very kind," Mena murmured.

She thought that she would eat her dinner quickly.

Then she would be able to slip into the garden without anybody seeing her.

She found it was a very easy thing to do.

Her supper, for she could hardly call it dinner, was delicious, but consisted of only two courses and some fruit.

"If yer wants anythin' else, Miss," the footman said who was waiting on her, "the Chef says as 'e'll do his best, but there's more to dinner to-night than 'e expected.'

"I have everything I want," Mena said, "and please thank the Chef very much for thinking of me."

She ate quickly, knowing the footman was in a hurry to get back to the Pantry.

As he carried away her tray she heard through the open door the sound of voices from below. She knew it was the guests moving from the room in which they had assembled before dinner.

They were going to the Dining-Room.

She wished she could watch them, but knew it was impossible.

It was a blessing that she was now free for at least the next two hours.

Without waiting to put on a hat, she went out bare-headed as she always did at home.

46

She found a secondary staircase and as she expected, not far from it on the ground floor, there was a door leading into the garden.

She let herself out.

The gardens were just as impressive as she had thought they would be from what she had seen from the window.

There was a large fountain.

It was throwing its water into the air so that it caught the last rays of the setting sun.

It rose from the centre of a beautiful carved stone basin.

Swimming among the water-lilies there were a number of gold-fish.

She went on through other parts of the garden until she came to an orchard full of fruit-trees.

From there she could see a paddock.

As she approached it she could see there were a number of jumps set up on the level ground.

She looked at them and realised that beyond them was the entrance to the stables.

She was just wondering if she dared to go and look at the horses when a man came through the gate.

He was riding a horse that was rearing and bucking.

Mena moved back a little so that she was in the shadow of one of the fruit-trees.

She watched with delight as the man struggled to control the horse under him.

She could see he was an excellent rider and had the same expertise her father had.

The horse was still fighting him, but not so determinedly as he had done at first.

Mena thought with a little smile that the man was winning.

She knew how satisfactory that would be to him.

The man then turned the horse round and rode him towards the first jump.

It was quite a high one, but Mena knew she could have cleared it easily.

The horse drew near to it at a fast pace.

Then just as he reached it he deliberately stopped dead.

At the same time he put his head down so that his rider could not avoid being thrown.

Although he struggled to keep his balance he fell against the fence.

The horse, delighted to be free of him, galloped away.

Mena gave a little gasp.

Then she pushed open the iron gate which was just in front of her and ran towards the fence.

The man was sprawled on the ground and she went down on her knees beside him.

As she did so he sat up and stared at her.

"Are you . . hurt?" she asked breathlessly.

There was a surprised expression in his eyes as he asked:

"Are you Aphrodite?"

Because the question was so unexpected Mena gave a little laugh.

"I am not as important as that," she replied. "I am only . . Philomena."

It was the sort of answer she would have given her father.

She spoke instinctively before realising that she had been indiscreet.

The Stranger smiled.

She was aware that he was an exceedingly good-looking young man.

He was wearing no jacket, and tucked inside the open-neck of his shirt was a loosely tied handkerchief.

"Philomena!" he said. "So I was not so far off the mark!"

"I was afraid . . you must have hurt . . yourself," Mena said.

"I might have," he replied, "but I was expecting him to do something like that."

The horse had not gone very far and was now cropping the grass.

"He is a magnificent animal," Mena said admiringly.

"That is what I think," the man answered. "But he is going to take a lot of breaking in."

He rose to his feet as he spoke and brushed the dust off his riding-breeches.

"Come and have a look at him," he suggested.

"I would love to," Mena replied.

They walked side by side over the ground towards the stallion.

He was certainly one of the finest horses Mena had ever seen.

"Have you had him long?" she asked.

"He arrived here a week ago," the man answered. "This is only the second time I have ridden him."

Mena thought the stallion must belong to the Duke and the man had been instructed to break him in.

The stallion looked up at their approach.

Then very gently Mena put out her hand to pat him.

To her surprise the horse nuzzled against her.

"He seems to have taken to you," the man said, "but perhaps you have the magic of your name."

She glanced at him questioningly and he said:

"Unless I am mistaken, 'Philomena' means 'I am

loved', and I imagine that extends to animals as well
as human beings."

Mena laughed.

She thought it extraordinary that anyone who appeared
to hold no more than a subordinate kind of position
should be aware of the meaning of her name.

Then she had a sudden idea and she asked:

"Did this horse belong to a woman before it came
here?"

The man thought for a moment before he replied:

"He came from Ireland and his previous owner was
the Countess O'Kerry."

Mena was still patting the stallion.

She realised as she did so that he was responding
to her.

Just as the horses in the stables at home appreciated
it when she made a fuss of them.

She turned to the man who was watching her.

"I have an idea which I would like to try to prove,"
she said. "Will you help me into the saddle?"

He stared at her in astonishment.

"Are you really suggesting that you can manage a
horse like that?" he asked. "You have just seen what
he did to me!"

"I think his behaviour was entirely due to the fact
that you are a man," Mena said.

"Why should you think that? And how can you, looking as you do, have any real knowledge of horses?"

Mena laughed.

"Lift me up!" she ordered.

"I will not be responsible if you break your neck!"

"I will take the risk."

Slowly and, she thought, reluctantly, the man lifted
her into the saddle.

50

She was aware that he was nervous and certain that the stallion would immediately throw her off.

She took the reins into her hands and now, talking softly she said:

"Now, take me for a little walk. There is no hurry, and you can, I know, be a good boy if you want to be."

The stallion twitched his ears as if he was listening to the sound of her voice.

Then she took him without hurrying down the centre of the paddock between the jumps.

The ground was smooth and flat and they reached the end of it.

She then turned back.

The man, who had come a little way with her to be ready to catch her if she fell, had stopped.

She walked the stallion back to him.

When she reached him she slipped to the ground before he could help her.

She patted the stallion and thanked him for the ride he had given her.

Then she looked at the man who was watching them both.

"There is your answer," she said. "He misses his mistress and resents you as a man taking her place."

"I was mistaken," the man said. "I thought you were a goddess, but now I know you are a Witch!"

"A White one, I hope!" Mena said quickly. "But I have to admit that my father once told me that he had had a horse who would never allow a man to ride him."

"It is something I have heard of before," the man said, "and I want to hear a great deal more about it. But I will first stable *Conqueror*."

"Perhaps I had better do that for you," Mena suggested.

She was still holding the reins.

They were walking towards the end of the ground where she knew the stables were situated.

Then just ahead of them she could see there were a number of grooms and stable-boys moving about.

She thought it would be a mistake for her to be seen by them.

She stopped.

"I had better wait for you here," she said.

"Why?" the man asked. "I would like to show you some of the other horses."

"And I would love to see them, but perhaps another time when there will not be so many . . other people . . about."

"Then wait here," the man said, "and I will come back."

He took the stallion's bridle from her and instantly the horse's head went up.

He seemed to resent the man being close beside him.

'I am right,' Mena thought as they moved away. '*Conqueror* is obviously on the defensive.'

She wished she could tell her father what she had just discovered.

'Papa would have been very interested,' she thought.

Since he had died there had been no one with whom to talk about horses.

In case she had been seen she moved a little way back in the direction from which she had come.

She was thinking there was nothing she would enjoy more than jumping the fences.

Sooner than she expected, the man was beside her.

She knew he must have handed over the stallion to somebody else to put him into his stall.

"Now," he said, "you have a great deal to tell me, and I am wondering where we can talk. Shall we go into the garden?"

Mena hesitated. Then she said:

"Is there somewhere where we cannot be seen from the house?"

"Yes, of course," he answered, "but why the secrecy? Or are you actually a goddess who had just arrived from Olympus to bewilder mankind?"

Mena laughed and it was a very pretty sound.

"How can you know so much about the Greeks?" she asked.

"I happen to have recently been staying in Greece," the man replied, "and I think your question is somewhat insulting."

The colour rose in Mena's cheeks.

Then as she looked away because she was embarrassed he laughed to put her at ease.

There was silence until he said:

"I am waiting for an answer."

"I thought . . perhaps you are here to . . break in the horses," Mena said hesitatingly.

"That is exactly what I do," he replied, "and now tell me your position."

I . . I am Companion to Mrs. Mansforde."

"Companion?" the man exclaimed.

Then in a different tone he said:

"Mansforde! Is she some relation to Lionel Mansforde who wrote those fascinating articles in the *Geographical Magazine*?"

Mena gave a little cry.

"You have read them?"

"I consider them the best description of the Ancient Greeks I have ever read," the man replied.

"I am so glad you said that. I know . ."

Mena stopped.

She was just going to say "I know Papa would have been thrilled," then she remembered who she was supposed to be.

A little lamely she changed it to:

"I . . I know Mrs. Mansforde would be delighted to hear you say that. He was her husband, but he died about a year ago."

"Died?" the man exclaimed. "I had no idea of that! He will be a great loss."

Mena drew in her breath.

She had thought that the series of articles on Classical Greece which her father had written for the *Geographical Magazine* were the best he had ever done.

"You must write a book, Papa," she had said to him.

"Perhaps I will one day," her father replied vaguely.

He really only made notes of what he had seen, and he wrote entirely to please himself.

"It was reading those articles," the man was saying "that made me determined to go to Greece, and I found them invaluable in helping me to understand all that is left there to see."

"I loved them too," Mena said.

Without her realising it, the man had led her to a part of the garden which was hidden from the house.

A small cascade poured down over some rocks.

It joined a stream which ran down the other side of the garden and eventually reached the lake.

By the cascade was a stone seat.

Mena looked at the water pouring between some strange plants which she was sure had come from lands overseas and sat down.

54

"Now I must know the rest," he said. "We know that your name is Philomena, and mine is Lindon."

"I like that name," Mena said, "because unlike my own, you cannot easily shorten it."

"I suppose that is true," he agreed, "but if, as I expect, you are called Mena, it suits you. I expect you have heard that before."

"From at least three-quarters of the people who have ever spoken to me!" Mena replied.

They both laughed.

She told herself that despite his gentlemanly ways Lindon obviously must be poor.

That must be the explanation for his taking the job of breaking in the horses.

"Should you be here?" she asked.

It was as if he followed the train of her thoughts because he replied:

"The penalty is worth the risk, and as you have just seen, I have learnt to take a fall without hurting myself."

"But you must be careful," Mena said. "And I am sure where *Conqueror* is concerned, it would be better if you let a woman make him more docile."

"Is that what you want to do?" Lindon asked.

Mena glanced at him before she said:

"It is something I would enjoy more than I can possibly say, but I am sure it is incorrect for a mere Companion to ride."

"I cannot think why," Lindon objected. "They eat, they sleep, they walk and doubtless dance! So is there any reason why riding should be reprehensible?"

"No, I suppose not," Mena agreed. "It is just that I cannot ask the permission of His Grace."

"There is no reason why you should," Lindon said. "I

am in charge of the horses, and therefore if you want to ride, I will arrange it for you."

Mena clasped her hands together.

"Do you mean that . . do you really . . mean it? You will not . . get into . . trouble?"

He shook his head.

"Then . . perhaps . . when everybody else is doing . . something different . . ?" Mena said tentatively.

"Leave it to me," he interrupted. "I imagine you are free from your duties after breakfast?"

"Later than that," Mena said, "I think my . . Mrs. Mansforde will have breakfast in bed."

"Well, as soon as you can escape, meet me at the top of the wood where I will be waiting for you."

Mena drew in her breath.

"Are you quite . . certain you will . . not get into . . trouble?"

"I am an expert at keeping out of it," the man said. "Now come along, and I will show you where we can meet. It is not far from here."

He took her along a twisting path through the trees. She found that the wood ended suddenly.

There were flat fields extending for some way ahead.

"It would be wonderful to ride there!" she exclaimed.

"Then that is what we will do," the man smiled.

As he spoke Mena was aware that the sun had disappeared over the horizon.

There was only a glimmer of light left in the sky.

"I must go back!" she said quickly. "Even if nobody else notices I am missing, the servants will think it strange that I am so long in the garden!"

"I will take you back," he said, "by a special route so that you will not be seen."

They walked without speaking.

56

Then as dusk began to fall they were outside the garden-door through which Mena had left the house.

"This is the way I escaped," she said.

"Now you know your way," he said. "I will be expecting to see you at eleven o'clock, and do not keep me waiting too long."

"I will try not to," she said, "but you do realise that I have no riding-habit with me?"

"Just come as you are," he said. "I am sure that goddesses do not dress up specially for riding, or for anything else they do!"

"If I am a goddess," Mena smiled, "then mind you provide me with a horse that is at least a Messenger of the Gods!"

"I will do that," Lindon promised.

He opened the door for her and as she went inside she stood looking back at him.

"Thank you," she said, "thank you very much. It has been very exciting meeting you and just what I expected in an enchanted Castle!"

"That is exactly what it is – now," he replied, "an enchanted Castle."

Mena met his eyes.

Then because she was shy she went swiftly into the Castle, shutting the door behind her.

CHAPTER THREE

Mena was asleep in the arm-chair in her mother's *Boudoir* when Mrs. Mansforde came in.

She opened her eyes and jumped up.

"Oh, darling," her mother said, "I told you not to stay up so late!"

"I have been asleep, Mama. Have you had a pleasant evening?"

"It was wonderful!" her mother answered. "It has been such fun and everybody was so kind to me."

Mena looked at the clock.

"It is very late for you, Mama."

"I know, but I have never enjoyed myself so much."

Mena helped her mother out of her evening-gown and did not bother to ring for the maid.

She realised that being with a party of people who had been kind to her had made all the difference to her mother.

Her eyes were sparkling and she looked years younger than when they had arrived.

"There are so many exciting things to do to-morrow," she said as Mena hung up her gown in the wardrobe.

"You have not yet told me what the Duke is like," Mena said.

"He is charming – absolutely charming!" her mother said. "If . . Lais . . marries him she will be a . . very lucky girl."

There was a little hesitation in the way her mother spoke which made Mena move to the side of the bed to ask:

"Are you afraid he . . will not?"

"He does not appear to pay her a great deal of attention," Mrs. Mansforde said slowly. "In fact I sat on his right at dinner and he talked to me for most of the evening."

"I expect he is sounding you out to make quite sure that Lais is the . . right person to be . . his Duchess," Mena said.

Her mother looked worried.

"I hope I did not say anything wrong, but he was so interested in Papa's work, and Mena – what do you think – ?"

Mena did not make a guess, she merely waited and her mother went on:

"His Grace is tremendously interested in gardens. I told him about our Herb Garden and how we could no longer afford to keep it up. He said he has one here and he is taking me with him to look at it to-morrow."

"That will be very exciting, Mama," Mena said. "I must try to have a look at it when you are all at dinner."

Her mother looked contrite.

"Oh, darling, I missed you, and it seems so unfair that you were not downstairs with all those interesting people."

"I have been quite happy," Mena said truthfully.

She would have liked to tell her mother about her

strange encounter with the man who had fallen off the magnificent stallion.

But she knew her mother would be shocked.

How could she be intimate with one of the Duke's staff?

She would also, Mena thought, be horrified at her riding surreptitiously without the Duke's permission.

She therefore tucked her mother in and said:

"Go to sleep, Mama. You look lovely, and you must go on looking lovely for Lais's sake."

"Good-night, my darling," Mrs. Mansforde said. "I love you, and I only hope that one day I shall be able to help you to marry the most charming man in the whole world!"

Mena laughed.

"I have to find him first!"

She blew out the candles by the bed and walked towards the door.

She let herself out into the corridor and hurried to her own room.

'It has helped Mama being here,' she thought as she undressed. 'She looks quite different!'

She only hoped the late nights would not be too much for her.

She hoped she would not be too tired in the morning to enjoy herself.

Mena need not have worried.

After she had eaten her breakfast and dressed she went to her mother's room to find she had just been called.

She was sitting up in bed eating a good breakfast.

She was looking, Mena thought with satisfaction, as young as she had last night.

"What are you going to do to-day Mother?" she asked when the maid had left the room.

"I am meeting the Duke downstairs at a quarter to eleven," her mother answered, "and he is taking me to see the Herb Garden."

She paused to take a sip of coffee before she went on:

"I am really hoping that no one else will be coming with us, so that we can talk seriously about herbs. He obviously knows a lot about them, and, as you know, other people are so stupid and do not believe herbs can help the sick as they have done for centuries."

Mena thought it was very satisfactory that the Duke and her mother should have something in common.

On subjects other than gardens her mother was inclined to be rather vague.

It was excellent news that her mother was to be downstairs by a quarter to eleven.

Lindon would be waiting and she knew of old that horses became fidgety if they had to stand about.

When she dressed, knowing she would be riding, she put on one of her full-skirted gowns.

It was in fact an old one.

There was no need to look smart for a man who did not wear a tie and yesterday was in his shirt-sleeves.

At the same time, she remembered he was very good-looking.

She expected there were plenty of women to tell him so.

She dressed her mother in one of her prettiest gowns which had been bought before her father died.

It was the colour of her eyes and there was a hat to go with it which was trimmed with small musk roses.

61

"You look a picture," she said when she had finished dressing her.

"That's true, Miss," the maid said who had been helping them. "We was sayin' downstairs that Madam's the most beautiful Lady as has ever stayed at the Castle!"

Mrs. Mansforde gave a little exclamation of surprise and Mena said:

"Now you know what people think about you! I have always said that you look like a flower!"

"Please," her mother protested, "you are making me embarrassed!"

She looked at her daughter as she spoke and asked:

"Why are you wearing that old gown? You surely have something better."

Mena gave her mother a little frown, and she said quickly:

"But of course if you have some work to do for me, there is no point in dressing up, is there?"

Her mother left the room and went carefully down the stairs.

Mena felt sure that the Duke would be waiting for her in the hall.

She now had to hurry to her own appointment.

She just took a quick glance at herself in the mirror to see that her hair was tidy.

Then she made her way quickly to the side-staircase and to the garden-door.

To her relief there was nobody about.

She hurried into the bushes where she would not be seen from the windows of the Castle.

It took her a little time to walk past the yew hedges and the cascade, and up through the wood.

It was the path that Lindon had shown her last night.

62

She only hoped she would not lose her way and be late.

She was almost breathless when she saw him standing in the shade of the trees with two horses.

She ran to him and as she reached him he said:

"For a woman you are surprisingly punctual!"

Mena smiled.

Then she looked at the horses and gave a delighted cry.

It was not the same stallion she had seen yesterday.

But one that was so outstanding that she could only stare.

It was without exception the finest stallion she had ever seen.

"I thought you would enjoy meeting *Red Dragon*," Lindon said.

"I have never seen such a marvellous horse!" Mena said. "Where can he have come from?"

"From Ireland," Lindon replied. "He and *Conqueror* arrived together, but *Red Dragon* is broken in so I do not have to do so much work with him."

"I have always heard that Irish horses are superb hunters," Mena said, "but I never thought they would look like this!"

"These are exceptional," Lindon replied, "and they have only been sold because their owner can no longer afford to keep them."

"It must have been an agony to have to part with them!"

"I am sure that *Red Dragon* will win some Classic races," Lindon remarked.

"Of course he will!" Mena agreed.

She patted *Red Dragon*, then looked at the other horse.

63

He was not so spectacular, but very attractive, being a grey with touches of white on his nose and fetlocks.

"Let me introduce you to *The Ghost*," Lindon said.

"Is that his name? I think it is a rather unkind one!"

"Not at all! Some ghosts, like the ones at the Castle, are kind and it is considered lucky to see them."

"Then of course I hope I shall be privileged to do so," Mena said.

Lindon picked her up and seated her on *The Ghost's* saddle.

"Now you look exactly as if you had stepped out of a picture," he said.

"If I am a ghost, perhaps I will step back into it!" Mena laughed.

"Not until we have had our ride," Lindon answered.

He sprang into *Red Dragon's* saddle.

They set off across the level ground galloping, but not strenuously.

To Mena it was a joy beyond words.

There were fine horses at home, but her father had never been able to afford a horse like the one she was now riding.

Nor the one on which Lindon was mounted.

'I wish I could tell Papa about it,' she thought.

They reached the wood and as the horses slowed down she said to Lindon:

"That was wonderful! I would not have given up this ride for all the jewels in Aladdin's cave!"

"And yet you would look very lovely wearing them," he said unexpectedly.

"Neither of the horses would notice that," Mena laughed.

"Surely, loving them as you do, you must have horses where you live?"

"Yes, of course," Mena replied without thinking. "They are not as fine as these, which are exceptional, but needless to say I love them very much!"

"So they are *your* horses!" Lindon remarked.

Mena realised she had made a mistake.

She had forgotten that if she was supposed to be working for a living she could hardly possess horses.

Because she could not think of what to say and did not wish to lie she rode into the wood ahead of Lindon.

As the horses passed between the trees he did not stop her.

She went on until she came to a clearing where the wood-cutters had been working.

There were logs cut from the trunks of the trees lying on the ground.

Kingcups made a patch of golden colour round a small pond.

"Let us sit down for a moment," Lindon suggested. "I want to talk to you."

Mena could not think of any reason why she should refuse.

She therefore slipped to the ground and knotted the reins together as he was doing.

"You do not think the horses will run away?" she asked a little nervously.

"*The Ghost* will stay where I am," Lindon answered, "and I am sure *Red Dragon* will do the same. Otherwise I shall have to walk home!"

Mena laughed.

"That would be a severe punishment!"

"But I could make you ride pillion, as women do in many different parts of the world!"

"Which would be distinctly uncomfortable if one had no saddle!" Mena said.

He smiled.

"That certainly is the answer, and I suppose you have read about it, unless in fact you have travelled."

"Only in my imagination," Mena replied, "but one day perhaps I shall have the opportunity of visiting the East."

"That is where you would like to go?"

"Of course," Mena replied.

She was thinking of her lessons in Oriental History and Eastern Religions.

"Yet I imagine," Lindon said, "your first port of call would be Greece."

"I have longed for years to go there!" Mena agreed.

There was a pause before she went on:

"When P . . Mr. Mansforde told me of what he had seen and found there, I knew how exciting it would be to stand beneath the 'Shining Cliffs' at Delphi and to walk round the Acropolis in Athens."

She spoke with a rapt little note in her voice because her father had made it so real to her.

"So you knew Mr. Mansforde," Lindon remarked. "How long did you say he had been dead?"

"A year," Mena replied after a little pause.

"And you were Companion to his wife before he died?"

Lindon was looking at her.

She knew he was thinking she was very young to be a Companion now, let alone a year or more ago.

"I . . I was not exactly a Companion then," she said quickly, "but I . . knew the Mansfordes and they were . . very kind to me."

She turned her face away from him as she spoke because she was blushing.

"How old are you?" Lindon asked quietly.

There was a pause.

"I have always been . . told that it is . . considered rude to ask . . a lady's age," Mena answered. "Anyway women are always as young as they look and as old as they feel."

Lindon laughed. Then he said:

"You are being very evasive, and I find it frustrating."

"I cannot think why," Mena replied, "and we can always talk about horses, a subject in which we are both interested."

"But they are not as interesting as you!" Lindon said. "I was thinking about you last night before I went to sleep, and it seems extraordinary that you should have dropped down out of the sky, that you look like a goddess, are interested in Greece as only a goddess could be, and understand *Conqueror* as I was unable to do!"

Mena put up her hands.

"What a lot of things to happen in so short a time!" she said. "I thought about yesterday evening and decided you were one of the best riders I had ever seen!"

"So you thought about me," Lindon said.

"How could I do anything else when you had promised to bring a horse today for me to ride? I was so afraid that something would prevent me from coming here."

"I think this is the sort of place to which you belong," Lindon said, "and now that I have seen you amid the trees and beside the pool, when I come here again you will undoubtedly haunt me!"

He got up as he spoke and walked towards the horses who, as he had predicted, had not gone very far.

Mena could think of nothing to say as she followed him.

He was certainly very strange in some ways.

She thought his slim, athletic figure must come from constantly being in the saddle and he was very handsome.

He was however just as casually dressed as he had been yesterday.

His shirt was clean, but again there was only a silk handkerchief round his neck.

His breeches were worn, but they were well-cut and, like his boots, were very much the same as her father would have worn.

"I am sure he is a gentleman who has fallen on hard times," she told herself. "It must be very frustrating to have to train other people's horses when you would much rather have your own."

The Ghost stood docilely waiting until Lindon reached him.

He unknotted the reins, then turned and lifted Mena into the saddle.

For one moment her face was level with his.

As she looked into his grey eyes she felt a strange feeling in what she thought was her heart.

Then she was in the saddle.

A few seconds later they were moving on through the wood, Lindon leading the way.

They galloped on flat ground until Mena said nervously that she thought she ought to go back to the Castle.

"Mrs. Mansforde may need me," she said, "and,

68

anyway, my luncheon will be brought upstairs early because there are a lot of people there."

"Do you eat by yourself?" Lindon asked in a surprised voice.

"Yes, I have it in the *Boudoir* attached to Mrs. Mansforde's bed-room."

"Why are you not downstairs in the Dining-Room?" he enquired.

"I am a Companion . . not a guest."

"That is no answer," he replied. "Governesses eat in the Dining-Room – at any rate for lunch – why not a Companion?"

Mena could not think of an answer to this.

She could hardly say it was because Lais did not want to acknowledge her as her sister.

"I am quite happy where I am," she replied as he waited for her answer.

"Then as you eat alone," he said, "I have a suggestion to make."

They were riding side by side and Mena turned her face towards him.

"What is it?"

"When Mrs. Mansforde goes down to dinner to-night, you come and dine with me."

Mena stared at him.

"How . . can I do . . that?"

"Quite easily," he answered. "We will ride to a place near here and I will try to make up to you for not being included in the large party eating and drinking themselves silly in the Dining-Room!"

The way he spoke made Mena laugh.

"I am quite happy . . upstairs with a . . book."

"And you think you would find that more enjoyable than dining with me?"

"No . . of course not . . but it is what I . . have to do!"

"There is no 'have to' about it," he said. "I want to have dinner with you and to talk to you without watching the clock."

Mena hesitated, then she asked herself what did it matter?

Both her mother and Lais would be horrified if they knew what she was doing.

But she was sure her father would have understood.

However lowly his position in life might be, Lindon was well-read and well-educated.

This last year she had missed so desperately the intelligent conversations she had enjoyed with her father.

She knew it would be an unmitigated joy to talk to Lindon.

She longed to be able to discuss Greece, or anywhere else in the world with him.

On Monday she and her mother would be going back home.

She adored her mother but she could not discuss any abstract subject.

Or even relate something exciting she had found in a book.

She had the feeling that when her mother returned home she would once again grow limp and listless.

It would be difficult to rouse her from her lethargy.

No one could really understand how dull and dreary this last year had been.

She made up her mind.

"If you . . really want . . me," she said, "it would be exciting . . to have dinner . . with you . . and also . . to ride there."

"Then that is what we will do," Lindon said. "It

would be easier for you to meet me in the paddock where you suddenly appeared yesterday. There will be nobody about at that hour."

"Then I will come," Mena said, "just as soon as everybody has gone down to dinner."

She saw the satisfaction on his face.

Then she said a little tentatively:

"Y.you do not think it is . . wrong of me? After all I shall . . not be . . chaperoned."

She had forgotten for the moment that she was supposed to be an independent and self-assured young woman who had to earn her own living.

"I promise you," Lindon said quite seriously, "that I will bring two horses who are elderly and will be perfectly prepared to chaperon you from the time you leave the Castle until you return!"

Mena chuckled.

"I can see them shaking their heads if I behave badly, and of course rebuking you for enticing me into . . mischief!"

"I shall behave with the utmost propriety," Lindon promised.

They were galloping back the way they had come and the sunshine seemed dazzling.

. . . .

Mrs. Mansforde told her that she had enjoyed a delightful day.

"You must see the Herb Garden, dearest," she said. "When I looked at it I felt ashamed that I have neglected ours for so long."

"We will weed it as soon as we get back, Mama," Mena said, "and what else did you see?"

"Orchids! Like those I used to wear in my hair, except

71

that they are far more exotic and unusual. And the peaches in the Peach House are already enormous!"

Mena thought there were a lot of things she must try and see before they left the Castle.

It was going to be difficult, however, if she spent all her free time with Lindon and the horses.

Her mother was obviously entranced with the gardens.

She did not ask Mena what she had been doing.

"In the afternoon," Mrs. Mansforde went on, "most of the guests went for a drive."

"Who did you go with, Mama?" Mena asked.

"The Duke took me in a very comfortable Chaise and Lais was with two young men who were obviously, I thought, very infatuated with her."

"Do you not think she had expected to be with . . the Duke?" Mena asked.

Her mother looked at her in consternation.

"I never thought of that! Was it wrong of me to monopolise him?"

"No, no, of course not," Mena said quickly. "You came here because he wanted to meet you, and he is very wisely finding out everything he wants to know about you."

Mrs. Mansforde smiled.

"I think he is charming, and I cannot imagine anybody I would rather have as a son-in-law."

Just as she had the night before, Lais came to collect her mother before dinner.

To-night she was wearing a flame-coloured gown trimmed with feathers.

Mena knew it must have been very expensive.

She had chosen for her mother a gown of pale mauve, the colour of Parma violets.

72

She looked very lovely with a glittering tiara on her head and wearing the same necklace she had worn the night before.

Mena remembered how Lais had said that her mother looked like a violet.

She thought however that if she too had gone down to dinner no one would have noticed her beside Lais.

"That is a fantastic gown, Lais!" she exclaimed to her sister.

"That is what I think," Lais said complacently.

"And your tiara is beautiful too," Mena added.

"Wait until you see me wearing the Kernthorpe diamonds!" Lais replied. "They have a tiara that is like a crown and strings of pearls which reach almost to one's knees!"

Mena thought that would be rather overwhelming, but aloud she said:

"I know you will look marvellous in them!"

Lais walked towards the door.

"Come along, Mama," she said. "I am very pleased at the way the Duke has taken to you, and you were very good to go with him to look at his boring Herb-Garden."

"I did not find it at all boring," Mrs. Mansforde replied, "and His Grace is actually very knowledgeable about herbs and flowers."

Lais was obviously not listening.

Mena kissed her mother before she left the room and whispered:

"Enjoy yourself, Mama, and do not forget to tell the Duke about the plants that Papa brought back from Greece."

"I had forgotten those," Mrs. Mansforde answered. "I am sure he will be very interested."

She hurried after her elder daughter.

As she disappeared down the stairs Mena saw a housemaid coming down the corridor.

She was just about to tell her that she did not want any dinner, then knew it would be a mistake.

It would seem strange.

Lais's lady's-maid would repeat to her everything she learned from the other servants.

She therefore waited impatiently in the Sitting-Room until the footman appeared.

A cloth had already been laid on the table and as he put down the tray she said:

"I have an urgent letter I have to write, so perhaps you would leave my dinner and come back to collect the tray later?"

"Yer quite sure yer can manage, Miss?" the footman enquired.

"Yes, of course," Mena smiled.

He hurried away, thinking it was a relief that he did not have to stay and wait on her.

As soon as he had gone Mena took off the covers.

She removed some of the food from each of the plates so that it looked as if she had sampled every dish.

She hid two peaches in the cupboard so that she could eat them later.

Then having made sure there was nobody about she slipped along the corridor and down the stairs which led to the garden door.

It might be wrong, it might be reprehensible!

But she was very excited at the idea of going out to dinner for the first time in her life alone with a man.

She let herself out into the garden.

Then she found her way as quickly as possible through the orchard.

74

When she reached the paddock he was there.

For a moment she looked at him in surprise because he was dressed as a Gentleman.

Then she realised that it was his informal evening dress, worn in some regiments.

It was in fact very much the same as her father had worn when he was a young man and a soldier.

Lindon's trousers, which fitted closely to his legs, had a red stripe down the sides.

She stared at him before she exclaimed:

"You are a soldier!"

"I was," Lindon replied, "and I thought this was the most appropriate way to be dressed when having dinner with a beautiful woman."

Mena thought he was probably excusing himself for not having the correct evening attire which he could not afford.

"You look very smart!" she said thinking it would put him at his ease.

"And you look very lovely," he replied.

She had put on one of her simple gowns.

It became her because it accentuated the curves of her breasts and her tiny waist.

It was not very low, but there were little puffed sleeves above her bare arms.

To make herself look a little more festive she had taken two of the roses out of a vase in her bed-room and pinned them in the front of her gown.

She had no idea how lovely she looked as the setting sun touched the gold of her hair.

Because she was excited her eyes were shining like stars.

Lindon stood looking at her for a long moment.

Then without speaking he picked her up and placed her on the saddle of one of the horses.

"What do you think of your chaperons?" he asked. "I think they will be needed this evening!"

It took Mena a minute or two to realise he was paying her a compliment.

Then he mounted the other horse and they were riding away from the Castle.

They moved in silence until Mena said:

"This is very, very exciting! I cannot believe there are many people who go out to dinner on horseback!"

"Not if they look like you," Lindon replied. "This is an adventure which I hope you will enjoy."

"I am already beginning to think that it is the most exciting thing that has ever happened to me!" Mena said.

Lindon did not answer.

He only urged his horse to go a little faster.

She hurried to keep up with him.

As they rode she wondered what was happening in the Castle Dining-Room to Lais and her mother.

She was sure it could not be as thrilling as what was happening to her.

CHAPTER FOUR

They rode in silence for about three miles across country until they came to a house surrounded by trees.

There was a drive which Lindon turned down.

It was not very long and at the end of it Mena gave an exclamation of surprise.

"It is Elizabethan!" she said. "Like my own home!"

She spoke without thinking.

Then she wondered if Lindon, because he admired her father, had any idea that her home was famous because of its age.

He rode up to the front door, dismounted and lifted Mena to the ground.

As he was doing so an elderly man appeared.

He touched his forelock and led the horses away in the direction of what Mena guessed were the stables.

There was a porch attached to the house and the same diamond-paned windows that she had at home.

It was however very much smaller than her father's house.

In fact when Lindon took her inside she found the tiny hall seemed almost overwhelmed by a large open fireplace.

Lindon took from her hands the shawl she had carried in front of her saddle.

He put it down on a chair.

Then he opened the door of what she knew would be the Sitting-Room.

Though small it was beautiful.

She realised at once that the furniture was all very old and fitting for the room.

Through a bow-window she could see the garden and knew at a glance that it had been laid out in the Elizabethan manner.

"This is lovely . . perfectly lovely!" she said. "I always think Elizabethan buildings are the most romantic of all!"

"I agree with you," Lindon said, "and what could be more appropriate for to-night?"

As he was looking at her admiringly Mena blushed and went to the window.

"M . . Mrs. Mansforde," she said stumbling as usual over the name, "was telling me about the Herb Garden at the Castle, and I was wondering if there was one here."

"Of course!" Lindon said. "But it is not kept up as well as I should like."

Mena turned her head to look at him.

"As *you* would like?" she asked. "Does this house belong to you?"

"It does, although I have been abroad for some time and it has been awaiting my return to care for it."

"Then you are very, very lucky to own anything so precious," Mena said.

"That is what I think," he replied. "Now come and have dinner and I will show you the rest of the house later."

They crossed the tiny hall and went into what Mena saw was the Dining-Room.

It was very small, but again perfectly in period.

In the centre of the room there was a round table with candles on it which Lindon lit.

"We are going to help ourselves," he said, "because there is no one to wait on us. But I hope you will enjoy the meal I have provided."

"How could I not enjoy being in such beautiful surroundings?" Mena asked, "And of course . ."

She was going to say "with you", then realised it would have sounded too intimate.

Instead she finished:

". . with . . somebody who likes the . . same things I . . do."

Lindon did not answer, but went to the sideboard.

There was food in dishes and plates on which they could help themselves.

"I am going to wait on you," he said with his back turned towards her.

There were two carved chairs at the table, the more elaborate of which was obviously Lindon's.

Although she did not say so, she knew they were not Elizabethan but Charles II.

This was because the carving depicted cupids holding a crown in their hands.

She sat down in the chair which she thought was meant for her.

Lindon brought her a glass of champagne, then poured out one for himself.

"This is a very special occasion," he said, "and so we are being extravagant."

Mena looked at him questioningly and he said:

"You told me this was the first time you had ever dined alone with a man."

"Yes, so it is very special," Mena agreed, "but I did not . . expect such . . beautiful surroundings!"

"The house was left to me by my father," Lindon explained, "and wherever I am travelling, or whatever I am doing, I like to think there is one place that is mine."

He helped Mena to the first dish and she found it was delicious.

After that, because they had so much to say to each other, it was difficult for Mena to realise what she was eating.

Ideas she had not been able to express for a long time seemed to flood into her mind.

She thought many of Lindon's replies witty and amusing.

They laughed a lot and the conversation seemed to jump from one subject to another, each one more stimulating than the last.

When dinner was finished they continued to sit at the table.

At last Mena said reluctantly:

"I . . suppose I . . ought to . . think of going . . back."

"There is no hurry," Lindon replied. "You know as well as I do that there is a big party to-night at the Castle and they will be late playing cards and dancing."

"Dancing?" Mena exclaimed.

"I heard," Lindon replied. "that there was to be a small Orchestra in the Ball-Room."

With difficulty Mena prevented herself from saying that Lais would enjoy that.

Lindon must have read her thoughts because he said:

"I am afraid that is something I cannot offer you!"

Mena laughed.

"As though I would want . . anything else . . rather than being . . here in this lovely . . perfect little house which is like . . something out of a . . dream."

There was silence. Then Lindon said:

"I wonder how many women, if they had the choice of living in something as large as the Castle or as small as this, would hesitate over which one to choose?"

"I think the answer really depends on whom they were with," Mena replied. "If it was with somebody they loved it would not matter whether the house was big or small."

"I wonder if you really mean that," Lindon replied.

There was a somewhat cynical note in his voice.

"Of course I mean it!" Mena answered. "And I think I would prefer a small house, just in case I lost the man I loved in a very big one!"

She thought Lindon looked at her in a puzzled manner and she explained:

"I remember my father saying once that whenever he took my mother to a party where she was greatly admired he hurried her home early because he was afraid of losing her."

"So your mother was beautiful!" Lindon remarked. "And of course you are like her."

"M . . Mrs. Mansforde used to say," Mena replied, "that the Greeks did not believe that a child was beautiful because of its father's or mother's features, but because of their thoughts."

She wondered if Lindon was interested as she went on:

"The Ancient Greeks had beautiful statues in the places where women went to have their children, and Mr. Mansforde believed that when they were with child it was from the very beginning that their thoughts and feelings affected not only the child's looks, but its whole character."

"I like the idea of that," Lindon said, "and I am sure that your children, when you have any, will be as lovely as you."

There was a deep note in his voice that made Mena blush.

She rose from the table saying:

"Please show me the rest of the house before I go, otherwise I shall always wonder what it was like."

"You are quite certain you will never come here again?" Lindon asked as he rose to his feet.

"We leave on Monday,"

She moved towards the door and he opened it for her.

There was a small carved oak staircase not unlike the one in her home except that this was very much smaller.

He took her up it and she found that on the First Floor there were three bed-rooms.

The largest, in which he slept himself, had a beautifully carved four-poster Elizabethan bed.

Mena gave a cry of delight.

"I wish . . Mr. Mansforde could have seen that," she said. "It is very like the one he had in his house, but has far finer carving!"

Again there was a bow-window with diamond panes which overlooked the garden.

The other two rooms had small casements and ordinary beds.

Each room contained a chest-of-drawers or a mirror which, even if not actually Elizabethan, fitted into the house as if made for it.

When they went downstairs to the Sitting-Room, Mena said:

"Thank you, thank you for showing me your . .

perfect little house. It is like a miniature and just as exquisite."

"That is what I hoped you would say," Lindon remarked. "And now I want you to admire this tapestry, then I will take you back."

The tapestry which covered one wall of the Sitting-Room was very old.

It depicted a wedding in medieval times.

"Where can you have found anything so attractive?" Mena asked.

"In Egypt, of all unlikely places!" Lindon answered. "They said it reached there at the time when Napoleon was attempting to occupy Egypt. I think, if the truth was told, it was stolen at one time or another from the French who were very interested in excavating the Pyramids."

"I want you to tell me about Egypt and the Pyramids," Mena said, "but . . now I must . . go back."

"Then your chaperons will carry us there," Lindon smiled, "and you can tell them that I have behaved with the utmost propriety!"

Mena gave a little laugh and looked up at him.

Then at the expression in his eyes she was still.

She knew what he was thinking; she knew what he wanted.

Because she was shy she turned quickly and walked to the door.

It was open and she went into the hall.

"Wait one moment while I fetch the horses," Lindon said.

He went out through the front door leaving Mena alone.

The sun was sinking and it was growing dark in the hall.

Yet she felt as if the house held out its arms to her.

It was the atmosphere, she thought, of age, but also of love.

She was sure those who had lived in this small house had been very happy.

It was the same thing, she thought, she used to feel at home.

She would hear her father and mother speak to each other with a note in their voices which was redolent with the love they had for each other.

She had been aware of it all through her childhood.

Only when her father died had she realised how much it had meant.

Now, strangely, she could feel it again.

It was as if the house not only welcomed her, but also spoke to her.

Then feeling it must be just part of her imagination she went to the open door.

As she did so she saw Lindon coming from the Stable leading both horses.

There was no sign of the old man who had taken them on their arrival.

"I am sure Lindon is too poor to be able to afford any servants," she told herself. "He must have spent most of his week's wages on the dinner and the champagne."

Because it was not as warm as it had been on the way to the little house, she put her shawl over her shoulders.

The ends crossed her breast to tie into a knot at the back of her waist.

She thought Lindon looked at what she was wearing and smiled as if he thought it sensible.

After he had mounted they rode off in the direction of the Castle.

He did not hurry. At the same time, he did not linger.

It seemed to Mena a very short time before they entered the paddock with the jumps.

They stopped at the gate which led into the orchard and Lindon said:

"I must see you to-morrow. What time will you be free?"

She knew as he spoke that she had been afraid he would not suggest another meeting.

It was something she wanted desperately.

"I would like more than . . anything else," she said, "to see the other horses . . in the stables. I have now seen four, and I am filled with admiration!"

"Then what I suggest I do," Lindon said, "is to show them to you at luncheon time. I expect the party will go round the stables, as they usually do, when they return from Church and before luncheon. After that there is not likely to be anyone there except perhaps a stable-boy or two."

"Then you will show me the horses?"

"As many as you want to see!"

"Thank you," Mena said, "and thank you, more than I can . . possibly say, for a . . . wonderful and most . . exciting evening."

"You were not disappointed?"

She laughed.

"How could I be? And I think your 'Dream House' is just as I describe it . . and full of . . happiness."

She was going to say "love", then quickly changed the last word.

"That is what I want it to be," Lindon said.

He dismounted and lifted Mena down from the horse she was riding.

He did not however take his arms from her as her feet touched the ground.

"I have kept my promise," he said in a deep voice, "and behaved as you wished me to, and I hope when you think of this evening you will commend me for my self-control in not kissing you good-night."

She stiffened.

Then before she could speak or move he had walked to the horses to pick up their bridles and lead them away towards the stables.

She stood at the gate watching him go, but he did not look back.

With a little sigh she turned away.

As she walked through the orchard she could not help thinking it might have been very wonderful to be kissed by Lindon.

Then abruptly she told herself it was something she must not think about – it was in fact very wrong.

There was no doubt in her mind that Lindon was a Gentleman.

He was exceedingly lucky to own such a beautiful house, however small it might be.

But he obviously had to work hard for his living.

She knew it would be wrong to have any man kissing her unless she intended to marry him.

"Lindon cannot afford a wife," she told herself, "even if he wished to . . marry me, which I am . . sure he does . . not!"

She knew too that her mother and father would be horrified at the idea of her marrying a man who, however good his breeding, was just a servant to the Duke.

"I must put him . . out of my . . mind," Mena told herself, "and perhaps it would be . . a mistake to see him . . to-morrow, even if it is . . only in . . the stables."

She reached the door into the garden.

Having gone through it, she was among the shrubs which would keep her concealed, until she reached the Castle door.

Because it was dusk it was difficult to see the path.

Mena was moving slowly along it when she heard the sound of voices.

She came to a standstill.

She realised that they were coming from the lawn on the other side of the rhododendrons.

There was the smell of cigar smoke and a man said:

"You are quite certain everything is arranged as I told you?"

"Your orders have been carried out exactly, M'Lord!" another man replied.

"What about the groom on duty?" the first man enquired.

"I've arranged that there will be a sleeping-draught in the ale he will be offered this evening."

"That is a sensible idea, Robert," the first man said. "Once we get *Conqueror* to France I will get a huge sum for him, and you will not go unrewarded."

"Thank you, M'Lord, thank you very much!" the other man replied.

"So many French horses were killed during the war with Germany in the Siege of Paris," the first man went on, "that those who want to breed only the best will pay high prices for good horse-flesh!"

"And Irish horses are exceptional, M'Lord!"

"That is what I thought myself as soon as I saw that stallion. So for God's sake do not make a mess of getting him away! The sooner you reach Folkestone, where my yacht is waiting, the better!"

"I'll not fail you, M'Lord."

"I sincerely hope not!" the first man said. "I will go in now. Good Luck!"

"Good-Night, M'Lord."

Mena knew the two men had parted, but she did not move.

She could hardly believe what she had overheard.

How could a guest in the Duke's party be plotting to steal *Conqueror*?

She was sure the man with the cigar was right.

The French would be only too eager to buy outstanding horses, and would pay large sums of money for them.

Then she knew that Lindon must prevent *Conqueror* from being stolen.

Walking on tip-toe because she was afraid of being discovered, Mena retraced her steps.

She went through the gates into the garden, crossed the orchard and arrived at the gate where Lindon had left her.

Then she was running as fast as she could towards the stables.

As she entered the yard she was relieved to see that the place seemed deserted.

The horses were all shut in for the night.

She was then aware that at the far end of a long row of stalls, one of the doors stood open.

She thought that must be where Lindon was stabling the horses they had ridden to his house.

She ran over the cobblestones, praying frantically that she was not being seen by either of the men she had just heard talking.

Then when she entered the stable she saw a movement in one of the stalls.

It was the horse she had been riding that evening.

In the next stall she found Lindon just removing his horse's saddle.

She slipped into the stall.

Hearing her feet on the straw he turned his head, then stared at her in surprise as she reached his side.

"Mena!" he exclaimed.

"Listen!" she whispered. "*Conqueror* is . . going to be . . stolen to-night and . . shipped to France."

He stared at her in sheer astonishment.

She realised he was looking at her by the light of a lantern which was hanging on a wall outside the stalls.

"It is true," she said, "I have just heard two men talking in the garden!"

Lindon took the saddle from the horse's back and carried it out of the stall.

He put it down in the passage outside, then he said:

"Tell me again what you have just said. It is quite safe! There is nobody else here at the moment."

Drawing in her breath Mena said:

"I . . I was . . just going . . back by the . . rhododendron bushes . . when I . . heard . . their voices."

She was stumbling over the words because she was so frightened.

She was so breathless after running so fast.

Lindon took her hand and held it with both of his.

"It is all right," he said gently. "Just tell me slowly exactly what they said."

"I was . . afraid I . . might be . . too late . . or that in trying to save *Conqueror* you . . might be hurt."

She thought Lindon smiled before he said:

"Try to remember every word."

Mena shut her eyes.

She was no longer trembling now that Lindon was holding her hand.

She found something very comforting in the strength of his fingers.

Her father had trained her to have a very good memory about what he read to her.

And after they discussed various subjects, she could recall every word he had said.

In making her report now, she did not raise her voice above a whisper.

When she had finished Lindon said:

"Thank you, darling, now I know exactly what to do."

As he spoke he put his arms around Mena.

Before she could open her eyes his lips were on hers.

He kissed her possessively and demandingly.

She felt as if he took her heart from her body and made it his.

Then almost before she realised the wonder of it he set her free and took her by the hand.

Because she was so surprised and at the same time thrilled by his kiss she could not speak.

She let him lead her across the cobbled yard and on to a narrow path bordered by bushes.

He stopped.

She realised she now was facing not, as she expected, a side-door but directly onto the front of the Castle.

There were the stone steps up which she and her mother had climbed on arrival.

"Go in that way," Lindon ordered, "and tell the footmen on duty that you have been for a walk by the lake."

He gave her a little push forward, then left her.

Almost before she could realise it he had gone and she was alone.

It was then she understood.

If she went in by the garden-door, she might be seen by one or other of the men she had overheard.

This way there was no possibility of anybody being suspicious if by some unfortunate chance she came into contact with them.

She forced herself to walk slowly and unhurriedly towards the steps.

Then as she climbed them she saw that the door was open.

There were two footmen in the hall.

They looked at her in surprise and she said:

"It is such a lovely evening that I have been for a walk by the lake."

"Oi' wish we could've done th' same, Miss!" one of the footmen smiled.

"Good-night!" Mena said lightly as she climbed the stairs.

"'Night, Miss!" they both answered.

As she went she could hear music coming from the Ball-Room.

She knew it must be some distance away.

She could also hear the sound of voices and laughter in the Drawing-Room.

'It must be quite a large party,' she thought.

But she knew that nobody could have had a more enjoyable evening than she had.

"It was . . lucky I . . went," she told herself. "If I had stayed here as I suppose I ought to have done, *Conqueror* would not have been missed until the morning, and nobody would have known where he was."

She was quite sure that Lindon would be able to frustrate the thieves.

Perhaps he would warn the Duke of what one of his guests had been planning.

She could imagine nothing more infuriating than for His Grace to find his magnificent stallion had been stolen.

Everybody would have admired him when they were shown the stables tomorrow.

'It was very . . very fortunate that I overheard those . . two men talking,' Mena thought.

At the same time she realised that on no account must she tell anybody where she had been.

'I am sure that is what Lindon would want,' she thought.

As she reached her bed-room she saw her reflection in the mirror.

While her hair looked a little untidy she knew, without being conceited, that she looked very pretty.

Her cheeks were flushed, her eyes were shining, and her lips looked as if they had been kissed.

"I always knew . . a kiss would be . . wonderful." she whispered.

Then she knew it was all the more wonderful because she had wanted Lindon to kiss her.

Also, although she was frightened to admit it, she found him very attractive.

Then as she thought about it she gave a little murmur of horror.

"I *must not* fall in love with him! That is something I must *not* do!" she told herself. "I will only make myself miserable, and when I go home I shall long to see him, which of course will be quite impossible!"

Once again she could feel his lips, strong, demanding and possessive.

As he had touched her she had felt something warm and wonderful come to life in her breast.

It was at first like the sunshine, or perhaps more like lightning.

Then it became an ecstasy beyond words and more thrilling than anything she had ever imagined.

She went to the window and pulled back the curtains.

Now darkness had fallen, the stars filled the sky and a pale moon was just beginning to rise above the trees.

It was so lovely, so ethereal and at the same time part of what she was feeling.

She knew that what she had felt in his little house was multiplied a million times by what she had felt at the touch of his lips.

It was no use.

However much she might fight and pray it was not true . . she knew that she loved him.

. . . .

It was a long time later before Mena turned from the window.

She told herself she must go to her mother's room so that she could help her undress.

At the same time, it was difficult to think of anything except that Lindon might be fighting with the thieves.

She was certain he would be sensible enough to have a number of men with him.

At the same time, there was a possibility that they would stop at nothing in their determination to steal *Conqueror* away.

She could only pray that Lindon would be safe.

Because it was growing late she hurried from her room to her mother's.

As she expected, her mother had not yet come upstairs.

Mena was just settling herself comfortably in the armchair to wait for her when the door opened.

Mena looked up expectantly, but it was not her mother who came in, it was Lais.

"Oh, it is you, Lais!" Mena exclaimed. "Mama has not yet come up."

"I know that," Lais replied. "and I am finding it extremely tiresome the way she is monopolising the Duke!"

Mena looked at her sister in surprise as Lais walked to the dressing-table.

She sat down on the stool and examined her reflection in the mirror.

She adjusted the tiara she wore on her head as she did so.

"Mama is only doing what you told her to do," Mena said loyally when her sister did not speak. "She says she likes the Duke very much and would welcome him as her son-in-law."

"But of course!" Lais said in a hard voice. "What mother would not?"

Mena did not answer and she went on:

"However, I want the Duke to myself, and I am finding it increasingly hard to get near him."

"We are going home on Monday," Mena said.

"And not before time!" Lais answered. "I saw a great deal of him in London – more than I have seen here – I can tell you that!"

"Perhaps we had better go to-morrow," Mena said in a small voice.

Then she realised that if Lais agreed she would not be able to see Lindon again.

She felt her heart contract at the idea.

"Of course you cannot do that," Lais said sharply. "People would think it strange. I felt sure William would pay me some attention to-night, but he has not even asked me to dance!"

"I . . I am sorry," Mena said.

"Actually I have had a proposal," Lais went on.

"You have?" Mena asked. "From somebody exciting?"

"I suppose most people would think he was," Lais said. "He is the Earl of Elderfield and, as it happens, extremely good-looking."

"How old is he?" Mena enquired.

Lais looked surprised.

"I do not see what that has to do with it, but I suppose he is about twenty-nine or thirty – and very rich!"

There was silence before Mena said:

"You do not . . think, Lais . . that you would be happier . . with . . someone nearer your age? And if the Earl is rich, you could have . . everything you . . wanted."

"I can buy that now," Lais said, 'but as I have already told you, Mena, I want the Duke!"

She spoke with a finality in her voice.

Mena knew of old it meant she intended to get her own way.

Then, because she thought it was the right thing to do, she made one more effort.

"Listen, Lais," she said, "we are sisters, and I have admired you ever since I was a little girl. You must have realised how happy Papa and Mama were, and everything that happened to them, even being hard up,

95

was magical because they were in love and so happy with each other."

She paused hoping that Lais was listening and went on:

"Surely that is what everyone wants! A title, however grand, would not make up for being bored and perhaps even . . disliking one's husband."

There was silence before Lais said:

"The trouble with you, Mena, is that your head is in the clouds and you have no practical common sense. A Duchess is a Duchess, and I would have a position in Society which will make everybody envy me and treat me with respect."

"But supposing you are . . unhappy with the Duke?" Mena asked.

There was a pause before Lais laughed, and it was not a very pretty sound.

"I shall have my strawberry leaves to console me," she said, "and I dare say a lot of other men as well."

Mena knew she was defeated.

She was shocked to think that Lais should consider consoling herself by attracting other men once she was married to her Duke.

Lais rose from the dressing-table.

"I am going back to the Ball-Room," she said, "and if Mama is still with the Duke I will take him away and send her up to bed. It is too late for old people to be up, anyway!"

She went from the room as she spoke, looking exceedingly lovely and very spectacular in her flame-coloured gown.

As the last feather disappeared through the doorway behind her Mena sat down again in the chair.

96

She felt as if her sister had brought something ugly into the evening.

Up to now it had been beautiful and enchanted from the first moment Lindon had lifted her onto the horse.

"I love him . . I love . . him!" she was saying over and over again.

The ecstasy he had made her feel was back again in her heart.

The love she had felt in his tiny house enveloped her.

CHAPTER FIVE

The Ball-Room was beautifully decorated with flowers and Elizabeth Mansforde looked at them with delight.

She had enjoyed the dinner-party enormously.

Practically every man who was staying in the house had paid her a compliment.

The lines had gone from her face.

She looked young and very attractive as the Duke came up to ask her to dance.

It was a soft romantic waltz and they moved slowly round the room.

Most of the guests were middle-aged.

There were however quite enough young married and unmarried women to look enviously at Lais, who was surrounded by men.

Her flame-coloured gown and her flashing diamonds made her undoubtedly the Belle of the Ball.

There was in fact very little competition.

As the Waltz finished the Duke said:

"I have something to show you."

Elizabeth Mansforde looked up at him and asked:

"More treasures? I find everything here so unusual, in fact unique, that I have run out of words with which to express what I feel."

"What I am going to show you now is something which I know you will appreciate," he answered.

They walked from the Ball-Room along a passage which led them eventually to the Orangery.

It had been added to the Castle at a later date, but was no less impressive for that.

The Orange-trees were just coming into blossom and at the end there was an extension which had been added by the Duke's father.

He opened the door and Elizabeth gave a little cry of delight.

It was an Orchid-Room and was very much hotter than the Orangery.

"I thought you showed me your orchids this morning!" she exclaimed.

"These are very special," the Duke replied, "and I was told while I was dressing for dinner that one which has been here for a year and which I had almost despaired of ever seeing in flower had produced a blossom to-night, in time for me to show it to you."

"How exciting!" Elizabeth exclaimed.

The Orchid-Room was quite small.

She noticed there was a comfortable seat with soft cushions on it.

Anyone who wished could sit there and admire the flowers.

The Duke took her first to where in the very centre of the other orchids was one plant isolated on its own.

She looked at it and gave a little cry of admiration because it was so beautiful.

"It is called *Laellocattleya*," the Duke said, "and it is very rare. In fact I doubt if any other collection in this country has it yet."

Elizabeth knew it was unique.

The blossoms were small, pale mauve in colour, each one exquisite in itself.

"It is lovely . . perfectly lovely!" she said. "Thank you for showing it to me."

The Duke drew her to the seat.

They sat down side by side looking at the orchids.

"I am thinking," he said quietly, "how beautiful it would look in your hair."

"But of course you cannot pick it!" Elizabeth said quickly. "It is far too valuable and you must just admire it as it is now and be very, very grateful for the privilege of seeing anything so perfect."

"That is what I thought I must do when I met you," the Duke said.

Elizabeth felt shy and kept her eyes on the orchid.

"What I am going to do," the Duke said, "is take you away from here to my house in Devonshire where I have been living."

"In Devonshire?" Elizabeth murmured in surprise.

"The house there is not as old as the Castle, but very picturesque and, I think, very comfortable. I have been planning out the gardens which I hope will be one of the most spectacular sights in the whole of England!"

Elizabeth drew in her breath, but she did not speak and the Duke went on:

"There is a great deal more to be done because I am creating not only an English garden, but also a Japanese one, which will be unusual, and my collection of orchids there is also very extensive."

"It sounds too wonderful!" Elizabeth exclaimed.

"I am also planning a Herb-Garden," the Duke continued, "and I desperately want your help."

100

"Of course . . I would . . like to help . . you," Elizabeth said, "but . . I do not . . see . . how . ."

The Duke took her hand in his.

"I am asking you," he said quietly, "if you will marry me!"

He felt Elizabeth's fingers tighten on his from the shock.

Then she turned her face to look at him, her eyes very wide and astonished.

"D.did you . . ask me to . . marry you?" she murmured.

"I fell in love with you the moment I saw you," the Duke said. "I had intended to wait, but I felt to-night when the *Laellocattleya* orchid came into bloom that it was an omen that perhaps you liked me a little."

"Of . . course I . . like you!" Elizabeth replied, "and I have been so . . happy every since I . . came to the Castle . . but . ."

She looked away from him and he felt her hand tremble in his.

He waited and after a long pause she said:

"I . . I came here because . . Lais thought you . . were going to ask her to be your . . wife."

The Duke smiled.

"A lot of young women have thought the same thing," he said, "but I am wise enough to know that while they want to be a Duchess they are not particularly interested in me as a man."

"I cannot . . believe that . . is true," Elizabeth said.

The Duke's fingers tightened on hers.

"I think, my darling," he said, "that you love me a little, even though you do not want to admit it."

He felt the little quiver that went through her.

"I was . . just so . . happy to be . . with you."

"Then that is all that matters," the Duke said. "I

101

am not interested in the Social World, and we can do our garden together and make it so outstanding and so beautiful that it will, in its own way, be a contribution to the glory of England."

He knew that what he said moved her and her eyes were shining as she looked up at him.

Then she looked away and said quickly:

"N.no . . of course not . . I could not . . hurt Lais and . . she would be . . very angry with . . me."

"I have a solution to that problem," the Duke said. "Elderfield was telling me to-night that he is wildly in love with Lais, and he would in fact make a very suitable husband for her."

"Do you mean . . the Earl? I thought he was a very charming young man," Elizabeth remarked.

"That is the right description of him," the Duke said. "A *young* man, and you know, Elizabeth, that I am old enough to be Lais's father."

"But . . I am sure she . . is in . . love with . . you," Elizabeth said miserably.

The Duke shook his head.

"She is dazzled by the idea of being the Duchess of Kernthorpe, of being *persona grata* at Court and, of course, being the envy of her contemporaries."

Elizabeth knew this was true and she found it impossible to deny what the Duke was saying.

At the same time, she asked herself how she could possibly accept the man her daughter wanted.

"What I am going to suggest," the Duke said, "is that you leave everything to me."

Elizabeth was just about to answer him, then she gave a little cry.

"I was thinking of Lais,' she said, "but I had forgotten something else which is terribly important and . . means

102

that however much . . I love you I must . . not marry . . you."

"Why not!" the Duke asked.

"Because the Duke of Kernthorpe must have an heir!"

As she spoke she thought she was deliberately destroying her one chance of future happiness.

At the same time she was sure she was doing the right thing.

"I thought you might think that," the Duke replied, "but I will tell you, Elizabeth, something I have never told anybody else. I mean the reason why I had no intention of ever marrying again."

Elizabeth looked at him and he saw the worried expression in her eyes.

He put his arm around her and pulled her closer to him.

She did not resist.

He knew as he had known before he spoke of marriage that she already loved him, even though she was not yet aware of it.

"My father married my mother when she was eighteen," he began. "It was an arranged marriage, but they fell in love with each other and their honeymoon was a very happy one."

He knew as he went on that Elizabeth was listening intently to every word.

"Shortly after they returned to live in the Castle my mother knew she was having a child. She told me later that she was very excited by the idea. At the same time, perhaps because she was so young, she felt very ill and found it frustrating not to be able to do all the things with my father that she wanted to do."

He paused before he went on:

"When I was born she had a very difficult time and, although she was so young, it took her a long time to recover."

"I was the same age when I had Lais," Elizabeth said, "so I know exactly what your mother must have felt."

"Two years later," the Duke went on, "my mother started another child. It was several years later that I began to realise that my father was frantic to have several sons just in case there was any difficulty about the succession. In fact, he became obsessed by the idea."

Elizabeth remembered how bitterly disappointed her husband had been when after Philomena was born she was told she could bear no more children.

He would therefore never have a son to inherit the Elizabethan house of which he was so proud.

"My mother had nine more children before finally my younger brother was born," the Duke was saying.

Now his voice sounded harsh.

"My mother grew weaker and suffered more with each child that was born. There were eight daughters, two of whom died at birth, three within a year of birth. The remaining three are married and, I think, moderately happy with their husbands."

Elizabeth could tell from the way he was speaking how much it had hurt him when he was old enough to be aware of his mother's suffering.

"It was only after my brother was born," he said finally, "that my father accepted what he had been told previously by the Doctors – that my mother must have no more children. But the damage had been done. She was never very strong and was very easily exhausted."

"You must have loved her very much," Elizabeth said softly.

104

"I adored her!" the Duke said. "And I would have done anything in my power to help her if it had been possible."

"It does . . not happen to . . every woman," Elizabeth murmured.

"I was married when I was twenty-four," the Duke said as if she had not spoken, "simply because my father was determined that I should provide an heir to the Dukedom. He chose my wife for me. Irene herself was the daughter of a Duke, and therefore completely eligible as regards the Family Tree."

There was silence before he went on:

"We saw very little of each other before the actual wedding, so it was not until we were on our honeymoon that we discovered we had nothing in common."

Elizabeth murmured sympathetically and instinctively moved a little closer to him.

The Duke's arms tightened as he went on:

"By the time the honeymoon was over and we came here Irene was expecting a child, but being very disagreeable about it."

He sighed as if he could remember all too vividly what had happened.

"She was determined that nothing should prevent her from doing what she wanted to do," he said, "and that meant riding. She was an outstanding horsewoman, but, I always thought, hard on her horses."

"You were . . beginning to be . . unhappy," Elizabeth whispered.

"I was unhappy because she defied me and insisted on going hunting, even though I thought that in her condition it was a great mistake to take high jumps and to ride horses that even I found difficult to handle."

Elizabeth looked up at him and he said:

"I expect you know the rest of the story. There was a great to-do about it at the time. She took a jump that was far too high for any woman and killed herself and our unborn child!"

"No . . I had not . . heard . . that," Elizabeth said. "I am so . . so . . sorry. It must have . . been a terrible blow . . for you."

"It was a blow indeed," the Duke said, "and it made me determined I would not marry again."

"But they tried to persuade you?"

"They did," the Duke agreed, "but I defied my father, and when that made him furious with me I went abroad."

"Did that make you feel any . . happier?"

"I found it extremely interesting," the Duke said, "and it made me determined that never again would I be subservient to anybody, or do anything that was against my own instincts."

"So you never . . married," Elizabeth said softly.

"I was determined not to, and I also, you will understand, hated the Castle and preferred to live in any of my other houses rather than here."

"So that is why I never met you," Elizabeth remarked.

"If I had met you and found you were already married," the Duke said, "it would have broken my heart! But now, my lovely one, I am asking you to make up to me for all the years when I have had nobody to love as I love you."

"Do you . . really mean . . that?" Elizabeth asked.

"You know I mean it," he replied.

His arms tightened. He bent his head and very gently kissed her lips.

He knew as he did so that he loved her as he had never loved anyone in his whole life.

She was everything he wanted in his wife.

She was feminine, sweet and gentle, compassionate and sympathetic.

He thought if they could be together among the flowers in his garden it would be all he would ask of life.

He had left Devonshire thinking he should pay his respects to the Queen.

He made an effort to take his place among his peers and carry out his duties.

But he found it all extremely boring.

It had amused him to find that because he was a 'matrimonial catch' he was pursued by all the ambitious mothers.

They paraded their daughters in front of him as if they were Yearlings in a Spring sale.

He was also amused by the invitations in the eyes of the Social Beauties who found him attractive.

They wished to add him to their list of lovers.

Because he thought he had been remiss in the past, he had made an effort to come to the Castle and give a party there.

Although he tried not to admit it, he felt as if the ghosts which had haunted him as a child were still with him.

Wherever he went, whatever he did, he was aware of them.

He appreciated that in his absence his Manager had kept up the garden in the same way that he had kept up the Estate.

But he knew, beautiful though this one was, his garden in Devonshire was far more attractive.

It owed its beauty not to the generations before him, but to himself.

107

As he kissed Elizabeth he felt he was kissing the flowers, especially the orchids that meant so much to both of them.

He knew that he would make the future for her as beautiful as they were.

The Duke raised his head.

From the expression of Elizabeth's face he knew that his kiss had meant as much to her as it had to him.

"I love you!" he said in a deep voice. "I love you so much that if you send me away I have no wish to go on living without you."

"Oh . . no . . you must . . not talk like . . that!" Elizabeth cried. "I love you . . I love you with . . all my heart . . I . . I thought I could never feel like this again . . but darling . . there is still . . Lais to think about . . and I am . . her mother!"

"If there were a thousand Lais's I would still make you marry me!" the Duke said. "But I would not have you upset! I am going to look after and protect you for as long as we both shall live. And I promise you that Lais will not be unhappy."

"But . . she will!" Elizabeth said weakly. "And she will . . never forgive . . me."

She could not help remembering that in fact she had not seen Lais since her marriage to Lord Barnham.

At the same time she thought it disloyal to tell the Duke how she had cut herself off from her family.

"What you are going to do," the Duke said quietly, "is to leave here early to-morrow morning before Lais is awake."

"L.leave?" Elizabeth exclaimed.

This was something she had not expected him to say.

"I intend to make sure she does not upset you, so

108

it is best, my precious one, if you are not in the Castle."

Elizabeth hid her face against his shoulder.

"I . . I do not . . want to . . leave you . ."

"It is only for a very short time," he said, "We are going to be married at once, and then I am going to take you to Devonshire."

Elizabeth drew in her breath.

"Is that possible . . is it really . . possible?"

"I will make it possible!" the Duke answered. "After that I will never allow you to worry about anything again."

Elizabeth seemed to melt against him and he kissed her forehead before he said:

"I find your tiara gets in my way, and if it stops me from kissing you I shall never let you wear one again!"

Elizabeth laughed.

"I would far rather wear your orchids in my hair."

"That is what you shall do," the Duke said. "I shall grow the most beautiful and perfect orchids which I will collect from every part of the world, just so that you may wear them like jewels."

Elizabeth gave a deep sigh.

"It sounds so wonderful, so perfect . . but . . oh . . William . . I am . . frightened!"

"I will not allow you to be frightened by anybody or anything," the Duke said. "Just do as I ask, and leave everything in my hands."

"You know I . . will do . . that,"

Then she gave a sudden exclamation.

"What is it?" the Duke asked.

"I . . I forgot . . I forgot to tell you that I . . deceived you when I . . came here."

109

"You deceived me?" the Duke asked incredulously. "How?"

"You thought I was . . bringing a . . Companion with me, but she . . is in fact . . my younger daughter . . Philomena!"

The Duke laughed.

"I had a slight suspicion there was something strange about your 'Companion'!" he said.

"Why should you have . . thought that?" Elizabeth asked.

"Because my Valet told me she was very beautiful, in fact almost as beautiful as you!"

Elizabeth smiled.

"She is far more beautiful than I am . . but she is only eighteen . . and I could not . . leave her . . behind."

"We will have to find a husband for her," the Duke said, "and of course, darling, she can come with us to Devonshire, as long as I can have you to myself and alone for just a few weeks after we are married."

"I promise you Philomena will be no trouble," Elizabeth said.

She gave a little sigh.

"I have, however, no wish to impose upon you. And you do realise we are . . very poor?"

"Well, I am very rich," the Duke replied, "so there is no need for you to worry about that!"

Elizabeth again put her head on his shoulder.

"Is it . . really true that I can . . marry you?" she asked. "I never thought of . . such a thing. I just knew you were the most . . charming and delightful man I had ever met . . and it would be . . wonderful to have you as a . . son-in-law."

110

"I have no wish to be a son-in-law or anything except your husband," the Duke laughed, "and that is what I intend to become."

He put his fingers under her chin and turned her face up to his.

"I love you!" he said, "I love you, and it is going to take me a lifetime to tell you how much!"

He kissed her until they were both breathless.

Then he said:

"It is getting late and as I want you to leave early, my darling, I think now you should go to bed."

"I will do as you tell me," Elizabeth said. "and I will dream of you, although I am afraid that in the morning you will have . . disappeared!"

"I will never do that," the Duke smiled. "And I am only sending you away, my precious, just in case anything upsets you. As soon as everybody has gone on Monday morning I will come to you."

"Promise you will . . not forget?" Elizabeth whispered.

He laughed tenderly.

"Could it be possible I would forget you?" he asked. "And I would like to think it would be impossible for you to forget me."

"It would . . it would!" Elizabeth said with a touch of passion in her voice.

Then he was kissing her again.

As he did so, the Duke was thanking God that for the first time in his life he had found the woman who was the counterpart of himself.

He had waited for her for a long time, it would make their happiness more intense and more perfect because they would be so grateful for it.

. . . .

Mena was not asleep when she heard the bed-room door open.

She had found it impossible to relax.

She had been wondering desperately what was happening in the stable-yard.

She prayed Lindon would not be hurt.

She had read stories in the newspapers of armed robberies taking place in London.

She remembered they had been crimes of violence during which policemen or one or more of the robbers had been killed.

She was afraid that the same violence might occur here.

When the thieves raided the stables to steal *Conqueror* Lindon would take steps to prevent them from taking him away.

There could be shots fired from both sides.

"Please, God, protect him . . please . . do not let him be . . injured."

She said the words over and over again.

She felt as if her prayers flew on wings to make a shield of protection around Lindon.

When the door opened Mena felt as if she was far away and had to come back from a long distance.

Slowly she got to her feet.

Then she was aware that her mother was standing just inside the room.

She looked so different from how she had before that Mena could only stare at her in astonishment.

Now she was standing quite still with her hands clasped together.

There was a look on her face that made Mena feel that something strange and wonderful had taken place.

When her mother did not speak she asked:

"What is it, Mama? Why do you look like that?"

"I am so happy, Mena!" her mother replied. "So very happy . . I cannot believe it is . . true!"

Mena walked towards her mother.

"What has happened?" she enquired.

Mrs. Mansforde drew a deep breath as if it was difficult to speak before she said:

"Oh, Mena! The Duke has asked me to . . marry him . . and I am going to be . . his wife!"

Mena could only gasp.

"*You* are going to marry the Duke? But . . I thought . ."

"He loves me!" her mother interrupted. "He had been determined never to marry again . . but from the moment I arrived here he knew he was in love! Oh, Mena! Mena! . . How can this have happened to me?"

Mena put her arms round her mother and kissed her.

"If the Duke will make you happy, Mama, as you used to be, then it is the most marvellous thing that could ever happen!"

"Do you mean that?" Mrs. Mansforde asked. "Oh, dearest, I would not do . . anything to . . hurt you or Lais . . but William said he had no intention of marrying her, or anybody else."

"If he loves you and you love him, then of course you must marry him!" Mena said.

As she spoke, however, she was thinking of how furious Lais would be.

There was no doubt about that after what she had said this afternoon.

She only hoped she would not have the disagreeable task of telling her sister what had occurred.

Mrs. Mansforde sat down on the stool in front of the dressing-table.

Mena began to take off her tiara.

There was silence until her mother said as if she had just thought of it:

"William says we are to leave first thing to-morrow morning before Lais is called."

"L.leave?" Mena questioned, "Oh, but why, Mama?"

"Because, dearest, he says he will not have me upset. He is going to talk to Lais and make sure she is not angry with me."

Mena thought that would be impossible, but she only said:

"I . . understand. At what . . time do we have to leave?"

"The carriage will be waiting for us at half-past-eight," her mother replied. "Our packing has all been arranged, and we will have breakfast in our rooms so all we have to do is to drive away without being observed."

Mena felt as if there was a stone in her breast.

It was so heavy she could hardly bear the pain of it.

She knew that once she had left the Castle it was unlikely she would ever see Lindon again.

How was it possible for her to explain everything to him in a letter?

It was then she realised she did not know his last name.

She thought perhaps she could write to him or send a message to the Elizabethan house in which they had dined that evening.

But he had not mentioned its name and she had not asked him what it was called.

She had also been very careful not to seem curious about his surname in case he asked hers.

After he had said he had read her father's articles and knew who he was, she thought she had been very stupid.

How could she have chosen the name 'Ford' for herself.

It would be all too likely for Lindon to suspect that, if she was not Mr. Mansforde's daughter, she was some relation.

'I should have ignored Mama's protestations,' she thought, 'and called myself "Johnson", as I first intended.'

It was too late now for regrets.

But it meant she now had no way of communicating with Lindon, or he with her.

As she helped her mother undress she seemed to be in a haze of happiness.

To Mena, however, it was the end of a dream, and now she had to wake up.

It had been a dream meeting Lindon and riding the horses with him, a more wonderful dream having dinner with him in his tiny Elizabethan house.

Then he had kissed her.

She had only to think of him to feel the pressure of his lips on hers.

Once again that strange, inexpressible ecstasy was rising within her.

Now she had to go away, and she knew it was something she would never experience again in the future.

She helped her mother into bed and kissed her good-night.

She was aware as she did so that her mother was immersed in her own happiness.

She would not notice anything else that was happening.

Mena went to the door.

"Good-night, Mama," she said as she reached it.

There was a pause, as if Mrs. Mansforde had to force herself to realise what was being said to her.

Then she said:

"Are you leaving? Good-night, then, dearest! And thank you for understanding how happy I am!"

Mena went to her own room.

When she reached it she ran in, shut the door and threw herself down on the bed.

Then the tears came, hot, burning, agonising tears.

She had found love – and lost it.

CHAPTER SIX

Lais finished her dance with the Earl of Elderfield.

He took her by the arm and they walked out of the Ball-Room window into the garden.

The night was filled with stars and there was a pale moon rising over the trees.

It was very romantic.

They moved over the smooth lawn until they were out of sight of the Castle.

Then the Earl said in a deep voice:

"You are looking very beautiful this evening, Lais, as I noticed all the other men told you!"

There was a note of jealousy in his voice which made her smile.

But she merely answered:

"I enjoy being here and the Castle is magnificent!"

"I have asked you to come and see my house," the Earl said. "It is not as old as this, but it was built by the Adam brothers, and you would look perfect in the huge Dining-Room and even more marvellous in the Ball-Room."

"I am far too busy at the moment to go anywhere," Lais replied complacently.

"But you came here!" the Earl argued.

"Of course," Lais replied.

There was silence until he asked:

"Are you going to marry Kernthorpe?"

Lais looked coyly away from him.

"That is not the sort of question you should ask."

"Answer me!" the Earl said fiercely. "I want to know the truth!"

"Then you will have to wait and see," Lais answered.

Except for the sound of the water falling from the fountain there was silence.

Then the Earl said in an almost despairing tone:

"You know I love you, Lais! And I could make you happy."

"How can you be sure of that!" Lais enquired.

"Because I am quite certain I could make you love me," he said. "There are so many things we can do together, and I want you! I want you unbearably."

He spoke with a harsh note in his voice.

But she merely gave a little shrug of her shoulders and turned away from him.

He reached out his hands and gripped her shoulders.

"Listen," he said, "I love you! For God's sake marry me, and give up pursuing a man who is determined not to be married!"

Lais stiffened.

"How dare you speak to me like that!" she exclaimed angrily.

"Admit the truth for once," the Earl said. "Kernthorpe is too old for you – much too old. Just because you think you want to be a Duchess, you are hanging round him like a lovesick teenager."

Lais struggled to free herself.

118

"You have no right to speak to me like that!" she cried. "I hate you!"

"If that is the truth," the Earl said, "then I will give you something to hate me for!"

He pulled her roughly into his arms.

Before she could protest or make any effort to hold him off his lips took possession of hers.

He kissed her fiercely, angrily and brutally.

It was impossible for her to move and difficult for her to breathe.

He went on kissing her until despite herself she was limp in his arms.

It was then his lips became a little more gentle, and he kissed her as if he wooed her.

Unexpectedly, so that she gave a little cry, he set her free, pushing her away from him.

"Damn you!" he swore. "You are enough to try the patience of a Saint!"

As he spoke he walked quickly away from her and disappeared into the darkness.

Lais stood where he had left her.

Her hands went up to her breast and she was aware her heart was beating tumultuously.

"How dare he . . behave like . . that!" she murmured.

Then, despite herself, she knew it had been exciting.

She went back into the Ball-Room but there was no sign of the Earl nor of the Duke.

Some of the guests were already leaving.

A number of the older women who were staying in the Castle were looking tired.

Because Lais was alone she saw a young man whom she disliked coming towards her and turned away.

She left the Ball-Room and walked along the corridor towards the hall.

She half expected the Duke to emerge from one of the rooms.

If he did so, she was ready to cry on his shoulder and tell him she had been insulted.

She felt then it would be difficult for him not to put his arms around her and say he would protect her.

What could his words be, after that, but a proposal of marriage?

There was, however, no sign of him.

She walked slowly up the stairs wanting to go to bed.

Yet at the same time, if she could find an excuse for it, she wanted to stay downstairs.

As she reached the top of the staircase several people came from the Drawing-Room who were obviously leaving.

While the men asked for their carriages a Lady, whose name Lais could not remember said:

"We must say good-bye to our host and tell him what a delightful party it has been."

"I have not seen him for some time," one of the men replied, "and it would be a mistake to keep the horses waiting at this hour of the night."

"Oh, very well," the Lady agreed, "I will write to him to-morrow and explain how sorry we were not to say good-night."

They were still talking as they went down the steps outside.

Lais moved to her room.

She rang for her lady's-maid, then went to the dressing-table to look at her reflection in the mirror.

She thought her lips were looking a little bruised from the Earl's roughness.

Then she was aware that her eyes were shining like the diamonds in her tiara.

Even her worst enemy would have to admit that she looked very beautiful.

. . . .

Lais stirred, aware that she had been awoken by her maid pulling back the curtains.

She had been dreaming and it was annoying to realise it had been about the Earl of Elderfield.

She had gone to sleep telling herself that she hated him.

She could not however restrain a little flutter within her breast when she remembered how angry he had been and how violent his kisses.

"There is no point in thinking about him," she told herself. "He is of no consequence in my life, and when we leave here there is no reason why I should see him again."

She knew, however, that when they went back to London he would not keep away from her.

Nor could she refuse to see him.

"He has gone too far!" she tried to tell herself.

She was thinking that he had frightened her last week.

"The trouble with you," he had said the first time he had proposed and she had refused him, "is that you are spoilt."

Instead of being offended she had smiled at him.

"How can I help it?" she asked.

"That is the trouble," the Earl answered. "Men pander to you because you are so beautiful, but what you

121

really need is that somebody should give you a good beating and make you behave yourself!"

She laughed at him.

Now her lips were bruised from his kisses.

She thought that if she drove him too far his threat might become a reality.

"He is quite abominable!" she murmured firmly.

Yet, at the same time, she knew she was surprisingly aware of how strong and masculine he was.

How helpless she had been in his arms.

She had ordered her breakfast to be brought to her bed-room.

She had no intention of going downstairs after a late night, as some of the older women did.

When her tray had been taken away her maid brought her bath into the room.

Two housemaids appeared carrying in large brass cans of hot and cold water which the footmen had brought upstairs.

The bath was scented with Oil of Gardenia which Lais always used.

Her maid rubbed her dry with a Turkish towel.

Lais dressed slowly in one of her most becoming gowns.

As she did so she told herself that things had gone far enough.

She was determined to see the Duke alone to-day, however difficult it might be to extract him from his guests.

"He has made enough fuss of Mama to last a life-time," she told herself crossly. "Now it is my turn!"

She had been determined not to leave the Castle without having accepted an invitation from the Duke to be his wife.

But she had not been able to have a single word alone with him, except when they were on the Dance-Floor.

He could hardly say "Will you marry me, darling?" when there were people milling around them.

All doubtless curious enough to try to overhear everything they said.

"I will say outright that I want to talk to him," she planned.

Her maid was arranging her hair.

When she looked at her reflection she saw she was looking very lovely.

She put a simple string of pearls round her neck.

It made her look young and not so sophisticated as she had looked the night before.

She thought the Duke would be impressed.

"I will tell him wistfully how very lonely I often feel," she decided, "and how sad it is as a widow to go back at night to an empty house."

A thought passed through her mind.

If she was married to the Duke, there might be many nights, since he was so much older, when they would sit alone at home.

Then she told herself sharply that if he had no wish to go dancing he was not likely to object if she went with a party.

She was so deep in her thoughts that it was with a start that she found she was dressed and ready.

Her maid was waiting for her to go downstairs.

She walked from the room and along the landing.

She reached the Grand Staircase with its magnificently carved banisters.

She thought she might be on the stage in a theatre, descending to the applause of the audience.

The only people in the hall, however, were two footmen on duty and the Butler.

As Lais reached the bottom of the stairs he came towards her.

She was about to ask him if he knew where the Duke could be found when he said:

"Good-morning, M'Lady! His Grace asked when Your Ladyship came down if you'd be kind enough to join him in his Study."

Lais felt her heart give a little leap of excitement.

He did want to see her!

He wished to be alone with her, just as she wished to be alone with him.

The Butler said nothing more, but led the way to the Study.

He opened the door and as Lais walked in he shut it behind her.

The Duke was sitting at his desk.

He rose as Lais appeared, smiled at her and said:

"Good-morning, Lais! I hope you slept well after such a late night."

"I did, thank you," Lais replied, "and I enjoyed the party very much."

The Duke came from behind his desk.

Lais seated herself on the sofa near the fireplace.

"I am glad you were able to come," he said, "as this is the first and the last party I expect to give at the Castle."

"The last?" Lais exclaimed.

"Yes, the last," the Duke repeated. "I have never cared for the Castle, and I came back just as an experiment."

"I – I do not understand!" Lais exclaimed.

"It is quite simple," he said, "I have decided that I

124

am going to retire and live permanently in a house I own in Devonshire."

"In Devonshire?" Lais echoed.

She thought as she spoke that she must sound very stupid to keep repeating what he said.

But she was so astonished that it was hard to believe what he was saying.

He sat down not on the sofa next to her, but on a chair opposite.

"I have not asked you here this morning to talk about myself," he said, "but about Michael Elderfield."

"Oh – the Earl!" Lais said. "I do not mind telling you he was very tiresome last night!"

"He talked to me after you had gone to bed," the Duke said, "and told me how very much in love with you he is, and how he wants to marry you."

Lais sat upright.

"He had no right to say such things to you, or even think them!" she said sharply. "I have told His Lordship I will not marry him, but he seems to be incapable of taking 'No' for an answer."

"I think you are being rather foolish – if you mean what you say," the Duke replied.

"Foolish?" Lais questioned.

"I have the greatest admiration for Elderfield," the Duke said. "He is very intelligent and a clever young man; in fact I am going to tell you something which is confidential, but I wish you to hear it."

Despite herself Lais was curious.

Although she wanted to tell the Duke she had no wish to continue to talk about the Earl, she felt obliged to listen.

"I intend to give up my post at the Palace, which as you know is a very important one," the Duke began.

"Give it up?" Lais enquired. "Why on earth should you do that?"

"As I have just said, I wish to retire," the Duke answered. "I am closing my house in London, and, of course you must not repeat this, I have suggested to Her Majesty that Elderfield should take my place."

Lais gave a little gasp.

She had made it her business to find out exactly how important the Duke was.

She was aware it was unheard of for anyone to give up such a position lightly.

"But, surely . . ?" she began.

"Her Majesty has been gracious enough to try to persuade me to stay on for a little longer," the Duke interrupted, "but I am getting old and I want to enjoy myself by doing the things I like best."

As Lais made no comment, he continued:

"I know that Elderfield with his enthusiasm and his intelligence will be exactly what is wanted, both at Windsor Castle and at Buckingham Palace. There is, however, one condition."

"And what is that?" Lais asked faintly.

"Her Majesty will not, I know," the Duke replied, "appoint anyone to take my position who is young as well as unmarried."

There was a pregnant pause before he added:

"As you are aware, Elderfield wants to marry you, and I cannot imagine that he would find anybody lovelier to help him and make quite certain his talents are appreciated even by the older men who will undoubtedly be a little jealous of him."

He smiled before he added:

"Just as their wives and their daughters will no doubt be jealous of you!"

126

Watching Lais, the Duke was aware that she was intelligent enough to understand exactly what he was offering her.

After a moment he said:

"I am quite certain that if Elderfield with your help and your encouragement is a success over the next few years, Her Majesty will then be likely to offer him a Governership somewhere in the Empire."

He knew Lais was listening intently as he went on:

"I was in fact offered a Governorship myself last year, but I refused. It was not what I wanted. But I know, Lais, that you would enjoy the pomp and circumstance that representing Her Majesty entails, and being treated as if you were in fact Royalty!"

He gave a short laugh before he said:

"You would certainly look very beautiful when holding Court."

Lais drew in her breath.

It seemed inconceivable that the Duke should be pleading the case of another man.

Yet she could understand perfectly clearly what he was suggesting.

"I am not trying to force you to make up your mind too quickly," the Duke went on, "but as you and I both know, there are bound to be a great many candidates eager for the position which I am vacating. If Elderfield does not stake his claim with the promise of being married, there will certainly be somebody else ready to get there first."

"I realise that," Lais said slowly. "But I had hoped . ."

She hesitated.

The Duke realised that she was about to say "you cared for me a little".

He could read her thoughts.

Before the words came to her lips he jumped to his feet.

"I do not want to seem inhospitable, Lais," he said, "but I have a great deal of work to do before the rest of the party who have gone to Church return. So you must forgive me now if I go to talk to my Secretary."

He walked towards the door.

"Incidentally," he said, "when I return to Devonshire to continue the work I am carrying out in the garden there, I have asked your mother to come and advise me about the Herb Garden. She is very much more knowledgeable about that than I am."

"My . . mother?" Lais questioned.

"I can imagine no one who would not only be so expert about it, but also who would enjoy it more!"

"And . . Mama has accepted to . . go with you to . . Devonshire?"

"I am very grateful that she has," the Duke smiled, "and since it would doubtless cause a great deal of gossip if we were there together for any length of time, she has made me very happy by promising to become my wife!"

He saw the astonishment in Lais's expression.

Then before she could say anything he opened the door and left the room.

For a moment Lais did not move.

She could only stand looking at the door.

She could not believe what she had just been told, or that the Duke was not joking.

It had never crossed her mind that her mother would marry again, let alone to the man she had chosen for herself.

"It is . . not true . . it cannot be true!" she murmured. "He must be . . joking!"

Then she knew it was not the sort of joke the Duke would make.

Nor did she find it in the least funny.

For a moment she thought she would scream from sheer fury.

"How could Mama have taken the Duke away from me?"

Then she was honest enough to remember that he had never been hers in the first place.

"But . . Mama . . Mama . . of all people will be the Duchess of Kernthorpe . . the Chatelaine of the . . Castle and a dozen other houses besides!" she told herself.

She would wear the Kernthorpe tiara at the Opening of Parliament.

Then Lais remembered her mother would not be in Westminster.

She would be in Devonshire talking to the Duke about his Herb Garden.

Doubtless thinking of nothing but flowers, and more flowers.

Lais had always thought when she had been at home that her mother's preoccupation with flowers was a bore.

She could imagine nothing she herself would wish to do less than to be isolated in Devonshire.

Away from London and all the parties in which she shone so dazzlingly.

Even being a Duchess would not compensate for having no one to admire her apart from the garden-boys.

At the same time she thought of what the Duke had just said to her about the Earl.

She could repeat it in her mind, word for word.

Of course that was the life she wanted.

To be of importance amongst Courtiers, Statesmen and Politicians.

To be respected by the Ambassadors who floated in and out of Windsor Castle day after day like a tidal wave.

She would also be present at all the Receptions and State Banquets which took place at Buckingham Palace.

She could see herself moving across the Throne Room.

When she curtsied to the Prince of Wales she would do it far more gracefully than any of the other women present.

Later she would be the wife of a Governor.

She knew exactly what that involved.

As the Duke had said, a Governor and his wife who represented the Queen in any colony were treated like Royalty.

Lais knew she would be curtsied to when she came into a room.

Michael and she would go into dinner first.

Again when people were presented they would curtsy and receive the Royal bow.

Suddenly she wondered if after what had happened last night the Earl had taken her decision as final.

Perhaps already he had left the Castle.

She opened the door and went down the corridor to the hall.

The Butler was no longer there, but there were two footmen.

"Have you seen the Earl of Elderfield?" she asked.

She had the terrifying feeling she would learn that he had already left the Castle.

Instead one of the footmen pointed through the open door.

"His Lordship be just walkin' down to th' lake, M'Lady,"

Lais followed the direction of his finger.

She could see the back of a man with square shoulders walking over the smooth green lawn.

She hesitated for a moment, then said to the footman:

"Give me a sunshade."

He produced one from under the stairs.

Lais walked out to the top of the steps.

She opened the sunshade and held it over her head as she moved slowly, but with a smile on her lips, in the direction of the Earl.

By now he had reached the lake.

She would not hurry, she decided, in what she had to say.

First he must apologise for being so rough last night.

At the same time, she had it in her power to make him very happy.

That was what she was going to do.

. . . .

The Duke's eyes were twinkling as he saw from the window of his Secretary's office Lais walking after the Earl.

'I ought to have been a Diplomat!' he thought.

He had known it would be impossible for anyone as lovely as Lais to bury herself in the country.

He had watched the expression on her face as he told her what he had planned.

Now he knew that Elizabeth need no longer be afraid of her daughter's anger.

At the same time he had every intention of doing what

131

he had told Lais he proposed to do: to resign his duties at the Court and retire.

He had already dictated a letter to the Prime Minister.

He had put forward the Earl's name as an excellent successor.

He had also written a very humble one to the Queen.

He had expressed his deep distress at having to give up the position which had given him the privilege of being in constant attendance upon her.

The letter continued:

> *"I hope I may have the honour and the great pleasure, Your Majesty, of coming to Windsor Castle occasionally. My wife-to-be is not strong and, on her Doctors' instructions, she needs to lead a quiet and restful life for a considerable time.*
>
> *I know that Your Majesty, with your warm heart and deep consideration for others, will understand my situation . ."*

He continued with a great deal of flattery which he knew the Queen always enjoyed.

Especially when it came from handsome men.

At the same time, he made it abundantly clear that it would be impossible for him to change his mind.

He then suggested with the utmost humility that Her Majesty might find an acceptable replacement in the Earl of Elderfield.

"*He has*," the Duke continued, "*just became engaged to marry my future stepdaughter, the beautiful Lady Barnham.*"

132

He realised it was a letter that would surprise the Queen.

At the same time, she was astute enough to know that he meant what he said.

His place would have to be taken by somebody else.

When he had finished the two letters, his Secretary, who had been with him for many years, said:

"May I congratulate Your Grace!"

"Thank you," the Duke replied. "However, Watson, this is for the moment entirely confidential."

"Yes, of course, Your Grace."

"And now I have a great many things I want you to do for me."

The Duke gave his Secretary a long list.

Then he went into the hall at the exact moment when a number of the party who had been to Church returned.

"I trust we will be able to see your new horses," one of the men said, "especially the Irish additions you were talking about last night."

"My stable-lads would certainly be disappointed if we did not make the traditional visit!" the Duke replied with a smile.

They followed him to the stables.

The Duke noted as he arrived that everything was in order.

There was nothing to show of the turmoil and excitement which had taken place last night.

He had been told about it first thing in the morning.

He learnt that while the thieves had fought fiercely to escape they had all been captured.

They had been tied up so that they could not move.

As soon as it was daylight they had been taken to the police-court in the nearest Town.

Long before any of his guests had come down for breakfast, the Chief Constable had called on the Duke.

Between them they had arranged that there should be no scandal.

Also, if possible, that nothing should appear in the local newspapers.

The thieves would be charged not with horse-stealing, but with the intent to burgle.

As they had dangerous weapons in the shape of pistols on their persons, they would undoubtedly receive a severe sentence.

The Duke made sure that a certain Peer who had been one of his guests was not mentioned.

He was however not surprised to learn that the gentleman in question had left very early.

He had told Mr. Watson that he had received a message that one of his relatives was dangerously ill.

No one however could confirm that any message had arrived at the Castle.

The Duke felt he could congratulate himself.

Everything was tied up neatly and satisfactorily and with no loose ends.

All he wanted now was to be with Elizabeth, but he knew he could not leave what remained of his party.

He also wished to make certain of Lais's engagement to the Earl.

He was able to ascertain this later in the day when the ladies went up to rest before dinner.

The Earl came to find him in his Study.

As he shut the door behind him the Duke thought he had never seen a man more happy.

"You know why I am here!" the Earl said.

"I am hoping my guess is the right one," the Duke replied.

"I have come to tell you that when I asked for your help last night I was in despair," the Earl said. "Now I am so happy that I feel I could jump over the moon!"

The Duke laughed.

"She *has* accepted you! I know you will be happy and she is very beautiful. Congratulations!"

"Thank you," the Earl said. "She is so beautiful that I am only afraid I shall be fighting duels every week or being sued for bodily assault!"

The Duke laughed again.

"I would not presume to advise you, but only a strong man, in the words of the novelettes, can conquer a beautiful woman, and that is what you will have to do!"

"I have every intention of it!" the Earl said firmly. "I shall be Master in my own house, and as you say, we will be ecstatically happy!"

"I expected to drink to your health," the Duke said, "and the champagne is already on ice!"

He walked to the grog-tray in the corner of the Study.

Lifting the open bottle from the silver wine-cooler which bore his coat of arms he poured out two glasses.

He handed one to the Earl and lifted his own glass.

"To your happiness, Michael!" he said. "May it grow and increase with every year that passes!"

"Thank you," the Earl replied, "and I understand I can say the same to you. Is it really true that you are going to marry Lais's mother?"

"It is true," the Duke confirmed, "but I have no wish to have people chattering about it before it takes place. We will be married quietly."

"I envy you," the Earl remarked. "I am sure that Lais will want a very large wedding so that she will be the

135

most beautiful Bride who ever walked up the aisle of St. George's, Hanover Square!"

The Duke laughed as the Earl went on:

"It really does not matter to me if I marry her on top of the Albert Hall or at the bottom of the Serpentine! As long as she is mine, that is all I want in the whole world!"

The Duke smiled as he raised his glass to his lips.

He was toasting Elizabeth.

'She is like an orchid,' he thought, 'so exquisite that I want her only to myself!'

CHAPTER SEVEN

Mena felt heavy-eyed in the morning because she had cried herself to sleep.

She had thought that not only would she never see Lindon again, but it would be a great mistake to do so.

How could she possibly tell her mother and the Duke that she was in love, madly in love, with one of his employees who looked after the horses?

She could imagine her mother would be very distressed.

The Duke would understandably be shocked and perhaps, because of her, Lindon would be dismissed.

'I cannot . . hurt him . . that is something I . . cannot do!' she sobbed.

She had gone to sleep murmuring his name and had awoken feeling as if he was near her.

Simply because she wanted him so desperately.

She washed her face in cold water and thought it made her look a little better.

She had no intention of explaining to her mother why she was depressed.

Nor must she in any way spoil her happiness.

As usual she carried her mother's breakfast-tray upstairs and set it down by the bed.

"Good morning Dearest," her mother said, "I have just been wondering if William will come to see me to-day. It seems a very long time since I saw him."

"I am sure he will come as soon as all his guests have left the Castle, Mama," Mena replied reassuringly. "Do rest, so that you will look beautiful when he does arrive."

She went downstairs.

Because she wanted the Duke to appreciate the house she went out into the garden to pick a basketful of flowers.

She arranged them in vases so that the Drawing-Room looked like a bower.

The fragrance of the roses scented the air.

She then went into the kitchen to see what Mrs. Johnson had for luncheon.

It was, she thought, very different fare from the delicious dishes they had enjoyed at the Castle.

Then she thought she must not be critical or make comparisons.

It was something she had told herself very firmly on their return when she had been to the stables to hug *Kingfisher*.

She knew as she did so that although he might not compare with the magnificent horses she had ridden at the Castle, he was delighted to see her.

She knew he loved her and as she hugged him the tears came into her eyes.

"I love you, *Kingfisher*," she said, "and however fine *Conqueror* and *The Ghost* may be, they could never mean the same to me as you do."

She thought *Kingfisher* understood.

He nuzzled against her and in his own way was trying to welcome her home.

138

She took him for a short ride in the afternoon.

But the beauty of the woods only made her think that Lindon was with her.

She hurried home because she was afraid of her own thoughts.

If it were not for the fact that it would hurt her mother and Lais would undoubtedly be horrified, she would have ridden back to the Castle.

She wanted to find out if Lindon still loved her.

He had seemed to do so when he had kissed her.

However, when she went to bed she thought perhaps his kisses had simply been an expression of his gratitude.

She had warned him about the thieves and had saved *Conqueror*.

Could he now wish to be with her in his adorable little Elizabethan house?

Before they met, he had been quite content with his own company.

He had said he had been abroad.

He had not however explained how he had managed to afford to do so.

She suspected that he had been employed by somebody.

Perhaps he had been a Guide or a Courier, for he was very knowledgeable about the different countries of which they had spoken.

Or perhaps he had been engaged as a Tutor.

Young men who were students at Oxford or Cambridge often engaged Tutors for the vacations.

She remembered how her father had said that travel had been so much easier than when he was young.

People of all ages, if they could afford it, now went abroad.

She could imagine Lindon would find some way of travelling even if it was not in comfort, or he had to work his passage.

Her thoughts kept her tossing and turning.

Finally because everything seemed so hopeless and she thought Lindon was as far away as if he were on the moon, she wept.

When her mother came down to luncheon Mena thought she was looking very lovely.

Her gown was not in the latest fashion.

It was one she had worn before her husband's death.

But it had been very much more expensive than anything they were able to afford now.

"You look very beautiful, Mama," Mena told her.

"Are you quite sure?" her mother asked. "Supposing when William sees me here rather than surrounded by the orchids at the Castle he does not . . admire me . . any more?"

Mena laughed.

"You would look lovely wherever you were," she said, "and I have always thought this house was a perfect frame for you. So are the flowers I have put in the Drawing-Room."

"That was sweet of you, Dearest," her mother said, "and I am very grateful."

As she spoke Mena knew that her thoughts were only on the Duke.

After luncheon she insisted on her mother lying comfortably on the sofa in the Drawing-Room with a cushion at her back.

She put over her legs an exquisitely-worked Chinese shawl.

Her father had bought it on one of his journeys abroad.

140

"Now relax, Mama," she said, "and try to sleep. Perhaps the Duke will be here at tea-time, so I am going to help Mrs. Johnson make some scones like those we had at the Castle, and also a sponge-cake."

"That is a lovely idea," her mother replied. "I do hope William will have arrived by then."

Mena was leaving the room when she thought of something.

"I wanted to ask you, Mama," she said, "what will happen to this house when you are married to the Duke? After all, we cannot just go away and leave it empty."

"You are coming with me to Devonshire, darling," her mother replied, "and I think the right thing to do would be to let Papa's brother have the house. After all, there have been Mansfordes living here for generations!"

Mena looked at her in astonishment.

"Give it to Papa's brother?" she said. "But he is abroad."

"I know, darling. He is in India with his Regiment, but when he wrote to me when Papa died he said he would soon be returning to England."

"Yes, of course," Mena agreed. "I remember that now."

She had been so deeply distressed by her father's death that she had found it hard to read the letters of condolence without crying.

"Stephen and his wife have several children," her mother went on, "and I am sure they would be very grateful to have a house in England after having been away for so long."

"Of course they would!" Mena agreed.

When she left the room she thought that everything was crumbling under her feet.

Now she was losing her home also.

The only home she had ever known and which she loved because it was so old and beautiful.

She knew too it would be uncomfortable to be a third person when all her mother wanted was to be alone with the Duke.

'Perhaps I can go away somewhere,' she thought despairingly.

She could think of no one who would welcome an unattached young woman.

She knew her mother would disapprove if she suggested trying to earn her own living.

"What shall I do . . what can I do?" she asked desperately.

There seemed to be no answer.

She and Mrs. Johnson made the scones and baked a cake.

Mena thought it bore some resemblance to those she had been offered at the Castle.

Then because time was getting on she went back to the Drawing-Room.

As she expected, her mother had her eyes closed and was asleep.

She shut the door very quietly and went out to the stables.

Kingfisher had followed her round the garden this morning while she was picking the flowers.

She now led him out of his stall again.

As she did so she said to the old groom who had been with her father for years:

"By the way, Gale, we expect a visitor later this afternoon. Will you be watching so that you can

142

look after his horses while the gentleman is with us?"

"Aye, Miss Mena, 'course Oi'll do that," the old man said, "an' Oi'll put some fresh straw down, 'case th' visitor wants Oi to 'tak' 'em from t'shafts."

"Yes, do that," Mena replied.

With *Kingfisher* following her she went into the garden.

However magnificent the Duke's garden in Devonshire might be she knew she would miss the one which was so much a part of her life.

She could remember when she was very small picking the first daffodils of Spring.

She carried them in triumph to her father.

"For 'oo, Papa!" she had said.

He had picked her up in his arms and kissed her.

"You are a very clever girl," he said. "You have brought me daffodils which appear when Winter has passed and Spring brings us new hope and joy and like Persephone sweeps away the darkness of Hades."

"Is that me, Papa?" she had asked, thinking the name was not unlike her own.

Her father had laughed.

"Yes, my dearest, it is you, and wherever you go you will bring the Spring to every man who looks at you."

Mena had not understood.

But she thought now she would like to bring the Spring to Lindon.

Then he could own his own horses and not have to train them for other people.

'Even if I . . never see . . him again,' she thought, 'I will pray for his . . happiness.'

She spent a long time in the garden, then took *Kingfisher* back to his stall.

It was nearly tea-time. She thought if the Duke was

going to arrive it must be soon because he would not want to have to hurry away soon after tea.

She entered the house to find that her mother was awake.

"I have been asleep," Mrs. Mansforde said. "Help me with my hair, dearest. I am sure it is in a mess."

"No, Mama, only crushed a little," Mena assured her.

Her mother rose from the sofa and went to the window.

Mena saw there was a worried expression in her eyes and she said almost beneath her breath:

"Perhaps he has . . forgotten me!"

Even as she spoke the door opened and Johnson in his best manner announced:

"'is Grace th' Duke of Kernthorpe, Ma'am!"

Elizabeth turned round and gave a cry of delight.

"You have . . come! You have . . come!" She said with the eagerness of a young girl.

The Duke walked across the room to take her out-stretched hands.

He kissed them, one after the other.

"I came at the very first opportunity," he answered. "I thought my guests would never leave!"

"But you are here!" Elizabeth said looking at him with adoring eyes.

"Yes, I am here, my darling," the Duke said, "and that is all that matters."

Knowing she was unwanted Mena had moved across to the door.

She was leaving the room when the Duke said:

"There is somebody outside to see you, Mena."

He just said the words, then turned again to Elizabeth.

It was obviously impossible for him to think of anything else.

144

Mena felt her heart leap.

Shutting the door she hurried across the hall.

Outside she saw the team of white horses that had carried her and her mother to the Castle.

Standing beside them and speaking to old Gale was Lindon.

Because she was so thrilled to see him she felt as if he was enveloped in a dazzling light.

He looked up at her standing in the doorway.

She thought that her heart flew from her breast and into his arms.

He had obviously given Gale his instructions for the old man started to lead the white horses in the direction of the stables.

Lindon came towards Mena.

He was looking very smart and there was a tall hat on his head.

She thought as he swept it off that he must have been driving the Duke.

Perhaps that was another of his duties.

As he reached her her eyes met his.

She was trembling because it was so exciting that he was there.

"I have to talk to you," he said in a deep voice. "Where can we go where we will not be disturbed?"

"In the . . garden," Mena replied.

Lindon put his hat down on the floor just inside the door.

He took her hand and they walked into the garden.

He did not speak as Mena led him to a special place she had wanted him to see.

It was a replica of a small Greek Temple.

Her father had bought it soon after he became obsessed with Greece.

It had been for sale at an Estate that had been broken up after its owner's death.

It had been an expensive purchase, and in order to buy it her father had pinched and saved.

Mena knew he loved having it in the garden.

In the Summer he took his work there and wrote undisturbed.

When they reached the Temple she knew that Lindon was smiling.

She waited for him to say something appreciative about it.

Instead he just took her into his arms.

He kissed her passionately, possessively and she felt as if the Heavens opened.

She was no longer on earth but flying high in the sky.

He kissed her until the ecstasy of it became almost unbearable.

With a little exclamation she hid her face against him.

He was still holding her close as he said:

"How could you do anything so damnable as to go away without telling me? I thought I would go mad when I found you had gone!"

"I . . I wanted to . . tell you," Mena answered in a voice that did not sound like her own, "b.but I . . did not know your . . name . . and although it . . sounded foolish . . I did not ask you the name of your house."

Lindon smiled.

"I thought it must be something like that. At the same time, I cannot tell you what I felt when I found you had gone."

"I was . . afraid I would . . never see you . . again!" Mena whispered.

He turned her face up to his and kissed her again.

Now his lips were gentle and very tender.

Then as he raised his head and looked down at her shining eyes and trembling lips he asked:

"How soon will you marry me, my darling? I cannot go on any longer without you!"

"Oh . . Lindon . . !"

Mena could only gasp the words.

The rapture and wonder of it seemed to seep through her body like sunshine.

Then she remembered how poor he was.

He saw the expression in her eyes and asked:

"What is wrong? What is worrying you?"

"I . . I want to . . talk to you."

"That is why we came here."

He drew her into the Temple where there was a sofa which her father had used.

It was worn and slightly faded, but still very comfortable.

They sat down and Lindon put his arm round her shoulders and pulled her close to him.

"You have not told me," he said quietly, "how soon you will marry me."

"I love . . you!" Mena answered. "I love you . . so much that it was an . . agony to have to . . leave you behind . . and I have been . . so unhappy . . since I came . . home."

There was a little break in her voice.

Lindon kissed her before she went on hesitatingly:

"You must . . know that I . . want to . . marry you I . . can imagine nothing . . more wonderful than . . being your . . wife. At the same time . . I cannot . . I must not . . hurt you."

"Hurt me?" Lindon enquired in a puzzled voice.

147

"What I am . . saying," Mena explained, "is that you have to . . work for your . . living . . and I am . . afraid I have . . no money . ."

"And you think that is important?" Lindon interrupted.

"It is perhaps . . possible for you," Mena said, "to live on your wages and keep your adorable little house but . . have you thought that a wife is . . an expense . . and . ."

She stopped.

"And – what?" Lindon prompted.

Mena hid her face against his neck before she whispered:

"S.suppose we . . have a . . baby?"

Lindon's arms tightened around her and Mena went on quickly:

"I would . . look after you and . . be as economical as I can . . but I could not . . bear it if I was just an . . encumbrance . . and you . . regretted marrying me."

She looked up at him and tears ran down her cheeks.

He looked at her for a long moment.

Then he took his handkerchief from the pocket of his coat and very gently wiped away her tears.

The handkerchief was of fine linen and smelled of Eau de Cologne.

Somehow because he was being kind it made the tears come all the faster.

He pulled her a little closer to him.

"You must not cry, my precious," he said, "there is nothing to cry about. But I love you because you are thinking of me, rather than yourself."

"I . . I am thinking of you because I . . love you," Mena said, "and just as I . . prayed on Saturday night

148

that you would not be . . hurt by the thieves . . I know I must not . . hurt you . . or in any way . . pull you down."

She was thinking as she spoke that to make money he might even take on more menial work than what he was doing now.

And if that failed, then he might be forced to sell his treasured house.

Then he would never forgive her because he had lost it.

The thoughts all passed swiftly through her mind.

But she was aware Lindon was looking at her as if because they were so closely attuned to each other he could read her thoughts.

There was silence before he said:

"I am just wondering, my beautiful and adorable one, how I can have been so lucky as to have found you, and how I can ever be worthy of a love that is so selfless and so part of the Divine?"

Because of the depth in his voice and the way he spoke Mena blushed.

"I have never known anyone before who could make me feel like this," Lindon went on, "but I know I want to kneel at your feet and light candles to you. At the same time, I can only express what I am trying to say with kisses."

He kissed her and Mena felt as though nothing in the world mattered except their love.

If they had to walk bare-foot and sleep under a hedge, at least they would be together.

She knew that without him she would rather die.

He raised his head before he said:

"I have already sent somebody to procure a Special Licence, and we will be married, my darling, to-morrow in the Chapel at the Castle."

Mena gave a little cry.

"M.Married at the . . Castle? But I have not yet told Mama about you . . and perhaps the Duke will not . . allow us to use . . his Chapel."

Lindon smiled.

"You do realise, my precious, that you do not yet know my name, or the one you will bear when you become my wife."

"It . . does seem absurd," Mena agreed, "but I did not . . want to . . tell you mine . . because I thought you might ask questions about . . Papa."

She knew the Duke must have explained who she was. Nevertheless she said:

"I came to the Castle as Mama's Companion because Lais had not admitted to anybody that she had a sister."

Lindon smiled.

"When you stumbled over your mother's name every time you mentioned her and you were very vague about your association with Mr. Mansforde, besides having a Greek name, I guessed who you really were."

"It is a good thing you were not able to say so to Lais! My sister would have been . . very angry!"

"I have news for you," Lindon said. "Your sister is going to marry the Earl of Elderfield!"

"She is?" Mena cried. "How wonderful! I told her he was the right age for her and therefore much more suitable than the Duke."

She looked at Lindon a little nervously before she said:

"You have been told . . or perhaps you have . . guessed that the Duke is going to marry . . my mother?"

"I know," Lindon replied, "and I am delighted about it!"

150

"It is so wonderful for Mama that she loves him. She has been a different person since we went to the Castle."

She gave a little sigh as she said:

"She has been so depressed about losing Papa and has had no interest in anything, but was just pining away."

"You must have been very unhappy," Lindon said.

"It was terrible losing Papa, and it has been very lonely here this last year when I had only *Kingfisher* to talk to."

"That is something you will never feel again," Lindon said. "I will make you very happy, my precious one. At the same time you will have a lot of things to do which may not be exactly what you want."

"I want to do . . anything that will . . help you," Mena said. "I will wash your clothes and scrub the floors as long as I can be with you and not . . lose you."

"That is something you will never do!" Lindon answered. "But your duties, my lovely one, are going to be very different from what you expect."

Mena looked at him nervously.

"What do you mean . . what has . . happened?"

She had the frightening feeling that he had taken on some new employment, perhaps abroad, or in London.

Whatever it was, it would mean that she could not be in his beautiful little Elizabethan house.

Perhaps, if he would be working all day, she would see him only in the evenings.

Lindon was reading her thoughts.

"It is not that," he said, "but because my brother is so intent on creating with your mother's help the most splendid garden in England, he has handed many of his responsibilities over to me."

151

Mena stared at Lindon in disbelief.

"D.did you . . say . . your . . brother?" she asked in a voice that did not sound like her own.

"I am Lindon Kerne," he answered, "and you, my precious one, will be the most beautiful of the Kerne Ladies who fill the Picture Gallery, and one day will be the most beautiful Duchess of Kernthorpe there has ever been!"

Mena had gone very pale with shock.

Now she hid her face against him to say almost inaudibly:

"I . . I do not . . believe it . . it cannot be . . true!"

"I can understand that you were deceived by my very unconventional appearance when I am working with the horses," Lindon said with a smile, "but I like to be comfortable, and I find a tie very restricting."

"You are laughing at me!" Mena said. "How can I have been . . so foolish!"

"It was not foolish," Lindon contradicted, "it was in fact the most marvellous thing that has ever happened to me."

His arms tightened as he said:

"You can understand that as the heir presumptive to a Dukedom I have been pursued by ambitious Mamas ever since I left the School-Room, and their daughters have wanted to marry me not for myself, but for my rank."

His voice deepened as he said very tenderly:

"You love me for myself, which has never happened to me before and although, my lovely one, you will not have to scrub floors or wash my clothes, we shall have a great many more responsible things to do which without you by my side I would find a bore."

"What . . are they?" Mena asked nervously.

152

"William told me last night that he has always hated the Castle, and he wants me to take it over together with the Estate and also run his race-horses which are kept at Newmarket."

Mena looked up at him.

"You will . . enjoy that!"

"Of course I shall," Lindon said, "and I know you will enjoy it too. At the same time, there will be a number of important duties we will have to perform in the County now, and I suspect a great many more later."

There was silence. Then Mena said:

"I . . I think because you will be . . so grand . . it would be a mistake for you to . . marry me."

It seemed extraordinary that she should be thinking of things the other way around.

She wondered how she could ever have been so foolish as not to recognise Lindon for what he was.

She had always been aware that he was a Gentleman, but she had thought he was 'down on his luck'.

"I will not have you frightened or upset," Lindon said, "and I think, my darling, because we love each other so much, that everything will be fine as long as we are doing it together."

"Of course it will," Mena answered, "if you are . . certain you should not . . marry somebody of more importance."

"I am going to marry you," Lindon said, "and as quickly as possible. I am only afraid that your mother will take you away with her to Devonshire, although I am sure that William will not want anybody else with them on their honeymoon."

He saw the light in Mena's eyes and said:

"And we want to be alone on ours. What I am

153

planning, my precious, is that we go first to my house where nobody will disturb us."

"Can we . . do that . . can we . . really do that?" Mena asked.

"We are going to do it." Lindon said firmly, "and as I intend to take a Chef from the Castle the food will be very much better than you had the other night."

"But it was ambrosia and the nectar of the gods!" Mena exclaimed.

She remembered that she had been so entranced she had hardly realised what she was eating.

He laughed.

"That of course is what you will find in Greece."

"In . . Greece?" she repeated.

"I am entitled to a long, happy and private honeymoon before we start being grand at the Castle!" he said.

"You are really taking me to Greece?"

"I thought we would go there and see you in your own setting as the goddess I thought you were when we first met. Then we will go to Egypt."

"It all sounds too . . wonderful to be believed," Mena said. "But . . anywhere would be Heaven if I was . . there with . . you!"

"That is what I have been thinking ever since I met you," Lindon said, "and now everything has fallen into place and all we have to do is to get married."

"And very, very quickly," Mena said, "otherwise I know I am going to wake up!"

Lindon laughed.

"I have arranged it for to-morrow morning," he said, "and William was talking of being married the day after."

Mena laughed.

154

"It all seems so . . impossible that I am . . breathless!"

Then as Lindon saw the light in her eyes she said:

"I know you are going to laugh at me for the rest of our lives because I thought you were a man employed to look after the Duke's horses, but why as you were at the Castle were you not enjoying the house-party?"

"Although William suggested it, the Irish horses had just arrived and I found the idea of being with them more enticing than his guests! How could I resist anything so alluring as *Conqueror* or *Red Dragon*?"

Because it seemed so ridiculous Mena laughed.

"Do you realise that if you had not been so enamoured of the horses and I had not come to the Castle in disguise as Mama's companion, we might never have met?"

"In which case," Lindon said seriously, "we would both have felt incomplete for the rest of our lives, and very lonely."

Mena put out her hand to hold onto him.

"You must be very, very careful of yourself," she said. "Those thieves might have taken you by surprise and I would have lost you."

"I have made quite sure that the horses will be properly guarded from now on," Lindon reassured her, "I realised I had been very remiss in not appreciating how valuable *Conqueror* was, or how vulnerable."

"I will try not to be frightened," Mena said. "At the same time, I love you so much that I shall be jealous of the horses if they take up too much of your time."

"We will train them together," Lindon promised. "I have never seen a woman ride as well as you do. And you quickly realised that *Conqueror* only responded to a woman rider."

"I am sure I can teach him to love you," Mena said.

"Then that is task 'Number One'!" Lindon answered, "and my task, my precious, is to try and make you love me more than you do already."

"I think that would be . . impossible," Mena answered, "but please . . please . . do try."

He gave a little laugh.

Then he was kissing her again; kissing her in a way which told her that he felt as she did that their love was blessed.

She knew that as they were married to-morrow their love would envelop them with a dazzling light.

She had felt it ever since she had loved Lindon.

It was the light which comes from God and is an expression of the love that He gave to mankind.

The love which is Divine and to which there is no end.

Other books by Barbara Cartland

Romantic Novels, over 400, the most recently published being:

A Very Special Love
A Necklace of Love
A Revolution of Love
The Marquis Wins
Love is The Key
Free as The Wind
Desire in the Desert
A Heart in the Highlands
The Music of Love
The Wrong Duchess

The Taming of a Tigress
Love Comes to the Castle
The Magic of Paris
Stand and Deliver your Heart
The Scent of Roses
Love at First Sight
The Secret Princess
Heaven in Hong Kong
Paradise in Penang
A Game of Love

The Dream and the Glory
(In aid of the St. John Ambulance Brigade)

Autobiographical and Biographical:

The Isthmus Years 1919–1939
The Years of Opportunity 1939–1945
I Search for Rainbows 1945–1976
We Danced All Night 1919–1929
Ronald Cartland (With a foreword by Sir Winston Churchill)
Polly – My Wonderful Mother
I Seek the Miraculous

Historical:

Bewitching Women
The Outrageous Queen (The Story of Queen Christina of Sweden)
The Scandalous Life of King Carol
The Private Life of Charles II
The Private Life of Elizabeth, Empress of Austria
Josephine, Empress of France
Diane de Poitiers
Metternich – The Passionate Diplomat
A Year of Royal Days
Royal Lovers
Royal Jewels
Royal Eccentrics

Sociology:

You in the Home	Etiquette
The Fascinating Forties	The Many Facets of Love
Marriage for Moderns	Sex and the Teenager
Be Vivid, Be Vital	The Book of Charm
Love, Life and Sex	Living Together
Vitamins for Vitality	The Youth Secret
Husbands and Wives	The Magic of Honey
Men are Wonderful	The Book of Beauty and Health

Keep Young and Beautiful by Barbara Cartland and Elinor Glyn
Etiquette for Love and Romance
Barbara Cartland's Book of Health

General:

Barbara Cartland's Book of Useless Information with a
   Foreword by the Earl Mountbatten of Burma.
   (In aid of the United World Colleges)
Love and Lovers (Picture Book)
The Light of Love (Prayer Book)
Barbara Cartland's Scrapbook
   (In aid of the Royal Photographic Museum)
Romantic Royal Marriages
Barbara Cartland's Book of Celebrities
Getting Older, Growing Younger

Verse:

Lines on Life and Love

Music:

An Album of Love Songs
sung with the Royal Philharmonic Orchestra

Films:

A Hazards of Hearts
The Lady and the Highwayman
A Ghost in Monte Carlo
A Duel of Love

Cartoons:

Barbara Cartland Romances (Book of Cartoons)
has recently been published in the U.S.A., Great Britain,
and other parts of the world.

Children:

A Children's Pop-Up Book: "Princess to the Rescue"

Cookery:

Barbara Cartland's Health Food Cookery Book
Food for Love
Magic of Honey Cookbook
Recipes for Lovers
The Romance of Food

Editor of:

"The Common Problem" by Ronald Cartland (with a preface by the
Rt. Hon. the Earl of Selborne, P.C.)
Barbara Cartland's Library of Love
Library of Ancient Wisdom
"Written with Love" Passionate love letters selected by Barbara
Cartland

Drama:

Blood Money
French Dressing

Philosophy:

Touch the Stars

Radio Operetta:

The Rose and the Violet
(Music by Mark Lubbock) Performed in 1942.

Radio Plays:

The Caged Bird: An episode in the life of Elizabeth Empress of
Austria.
Performed in 1957.

A List of Barbara Cartland Titles Available from Mandarin

While every effort is made to keep prices low, it is sometimes necessary to increase prices at short notice. Mandarin Paperbacks reserves the right to show new retail prices on covers which may differ from those previously advertised in the text or elsewhere.

The prices shown below were correct at the time of going to press.

☐	7493 0745 5	**Magic from the Heart**	£2.99
☐	7493 0746 3	**Two Hearts in Hungary**	£2.99
☐	7493 0743 9	**Too Precious to Lose**	£2.99
☐	7493 0744 7	**A Theatre of Love**	£2.99
☐	7493 0841 9	**Love is the Key**	£2.99
☐	7493 0838 9	**The Magic of Paris**	£2.99
☐	7493 0832 X	**Stand and Deliver Your Heart**	£2.99
☐	7493 0833 8	**The Scent of Roses**	£2.99

All these books are available at your bookshop or newsagent, or can be ordered direct from the publisher. Just tick the titles you want and fill in the form below.

Mandarin Paperbacks, Cash Sales Department, PO Box 11, Falmouth, Cornwall TR10 9EN.

Please send cheque or postal order, no currency, for purchase price quoted and allow the following for postage and packing:

UK	80p for the first book, 20p for each additional book ordered to a maximum charge of £2.00.
BFPO	80p for the first book, 20p for each additional book.
Overseas including Eire	£1.50 for the first book, £1.00 for the second and 30p for each additional book thereafter.

NAME (Block letters) ....

ADDRESS ....

....

☐ I enclose my remittance for ....

☐ I wish to pay by Access/Visa Card Number ☐☐☐☐☐☐☐☐☐☐☐☐☐☐☐☐

Expiry Date ☐☐☐☐